NECESSARY RISK

VANISHING RANCH
BOOK 2

CHRISTY BARRITT

CHAPTER
ONE

HUDSON CARMICHAEL HAD ONLY one chance to complete this mission.

His objective: grab Kat Farino and flee.

Failure wasn't an option.

Otherwise, mob boss Frank Farino would kill her. Kat was Frank's daughter-in-law, a young widow whose life depended on getting away from the volatile family she'd married into.

Hudson had studied Kat's file. He knew what she looked like. Knew what kind of danger she faced. Knew he had one chance to save her.

Darkness cast shadows around Hudson as he lingered on a street corner in downtown Dallas, Texas. The summer heat was nearly oppressive, even in the evening, and it made him appreciate the dry climate of Arizona, where he now lived.

Kat was shopping at an upscale department store,

two bodyguards with her. Another two of Farino's men were positioned down the street.

They clearly didn't want to let her out of their sight.

Hudson couldn't imagine what kind of life that might be.

Kat knew someone from a rescue organization was coming.

But not who. Not when. Not where.

Too many people couldn't keep a secret. Couldn't hide the truth when they knew something was about to happen.

The element of surprise was essential.

Hudson smiled and tipped his head at a woman who walked past him. He tried to look casual, like he had a reason to stand here—to admire the ladies heading to one of many bars or clubs in the area.

But it was all an act.

Subterfuge was a part of his job description.

He glanced at his watch.

The store should be closing soon, which meant Kat should emerge any minute.

He scoped out the area again as he waited.

Farino's men were close.

But Hudson knew how to handle this.

Footsteps sounded in the distance, and he glanced back.

It was her.

Kat.

She left the store, carrying three bags on one arm and a designer purse on the other.

Her two bodyguards weren't beside her.

Were they grabbing the car?

He didn't know.

But this was his chance.

Hudson began his approach, trying to look casual as he strolled toward the store.

He'd seen the pictures of the woman with her bleached blonde hair, slim build, and immaculate makeup. He'd seen her brown eyes, aloof expression, and pert nose.

But seeing Kat in person stopped him in his tracks.

The photos didn't reveal the surprising depth of her gaze. How she walked. Her brisk, fluid motions.

Those mannerisms . . . they were unmistakable.

Kat Farino looked and moved almost exactly like Teagan Murphy . . . his dead fiancée.

Kat spotted him and froze.

Was that recognition flickering in her gaze?

Or was Hudson imagining things and seeing what he wanted to see?

———

Kat's heart thrummed in her ears when she saw the man standing in front of her.

No . . . it couldn't be.

But she knew it was.

Hudson Carmichael.

She'd thought about him every day for the past two years.

And now he was here.

Standing in front of her.

Looking just as stupefied as she felt.

As a horn sounded in the distance, she snapped back to reality and remembered her new persona.

She couldn't let Hudson know she recognized him.

It wouldn't be safe. For either of them.

Her heart thumped harder at the thought.

Her life depended on her ability to blend in, to stay below the radar.

But she'd seen Hudson, and now her bones felt like they might crumble right along with her resolve.

"Teagan?" He stared at her, a knot between his eyes.

She raised her chin and glanced around. Richard and Felix had stopped just inside the door to answer the boss's phone call. She hoped they didn't emerge and see this conversation.

And what was Hudson even doing here? His motions didn't indicate this meeting was an accident . . . yet he seemed confused to see her.

"You must have me mistaken for someone else." Her voice sounded raw, even to her own ears.

She tried to push past him.

Hudson grabbed her arm, his gaze boring into hers. "No, I didn't."

"I'm sorry, but—"

"We don't have time to play games." His voice came out low and demanding, leaving no room for questions.

She tried to pull away, but he wouldn't release her. "What are you doing?"

"I'm your ride. We need to go. Now—before those buffoons flanking you return."

She swallowed hard as realizations filled her mind. "You're the one who came to rescue me?"

Hudson gave her another hard stare before nodding. "That's me. We need to get you out of here. Now." He glanced over his shoulder. "Frank has his guys watching."

Just as Hudson said the words, a car careened down the road toward them, and the two bodyguards emerged from the store.

"I think we're too late," Teagan whispered.

Hudson's jaw hardened. "No, we're not. Come on. Let's get out of here."

CHAPTER
TWO

HUDSON'S MIND wouldn't stop racing.

This woman with him was Teagan Murphy.

He was certain of it.

But . . . Teagan was dead. She'd died in a plane crash on her way to Brazil for a business trip two years ago. He'd had a funeral for her. He visited her grave every month.

An ache formed in his chest at the thought.

There was no time to think about his loss now.

He had to move.

Gripping Kat's—Teagan's—arm, Hudson raced forward, pulling her toward a parking garage the next block over.

He shouldn't have allowed himself to get distracted. But he hadn't foreseen this turn of events.

Still . . . he was a trained warrior. A former Navy SEAL. He'd been taught how to separate himself from his emotions.

That was exactly what he had to do right now.

He and Teagan would have time to talk later.

First, they needed to get to safety.

"Hudson . . ." Teagan murmured as they ran through the alley.

There it was.

Proof she was Teagan.

Because he hadn't told her his name.

Delight and confusion clashed inside him.

He'd have time to deal with those emotions later.

Right now, a car squealed behind them.

Footsteps pounded on their heels.

With four armed men after them, they couldn't risk getting caught.

They had to get away.

"My SUV's right up here," he muttered. "We can make it."

"Who's with you?" She sounded nearly breathless with anxiety.

"Just me."

"Just you?" Her voice lilted close to a screech. "I thought you guys were professionals."

"We are."

They reached the garage and darted inside. Still pulling her beside him, Hudson led her around cars as they raced through the space.

But this wasn't where he parked.

Coming here had only been a distraction, a way of buying time. Getting through the gate at the entrance of the garage would slow down the guys in the car.

The guys chasing them on foot?

They could be a different story.

He hoped the decision paid off.

Hudson glanced behind him again.

He was about to find out.

Teagan could hardly breathe.

Too many thoughts raced through her mind.

Too many fears.

Each jab of anxiety nearly froze her.

But she couldn't let fear win. It had already been winning for entirely too long.

If her father-in-law's men got to them, Hudson would die. Teagan would be as good as dead.

She tried to ignore the fire racing through her as Hudson gripped her arm.

He was never supposed to be back in her real life again.

Only in her dreams. But those had seemed so heart-wrenchingly unreachable that they'd only brought her pain. She'd tried to suffocate any hopes she had of seeing him again.

Especially not like this.

As they darted through the parking garage, gunfire echoed behind them.

She sucked in a breath.

They were shooting.

Her in-law's henchmen were *shooting*.

At her? At Hudson? Or both?

She wasn't sure.

"Keep moving!" Hudson yelled. "We can't slow down."

Teagan didn't have time to ask any questions. To think. To contemplate.

They only had time to do.

Hudson turned and pulled her down a set of stairs —even though they'd just come up a different set.

As they did, a man rushed from below.

Felix.

She sucked in her breath, a hand going over her stomach as she felt nausea gurgling inside her.

Hudson threw an arm back to push her out of the way. Then he swung his leg.

His foot hit Felix's gun, and the Glock went flying through the air.

Felix scowled, clearly unhappy.

He let out a grunt before charging Hudson.

But Hudson was too quick.

He ducked, and Felix smashed into the cement wall.

The next instant, Hudson's fist hit Felix's jaw.

Felix reeled backward, tumbling down a few steps and landing on his back.

Wasting no time, Hudson rushed toward the man.

Before he could gather himself, Hudson put the man in a chokehold and waited until his body went limp as he passed out.

He'd be out of commission for a few minutes at least.

"Come on!" Hudson held out his hand.

Teagan stared at it a moment.

She'd always known he was a trained fighter. But she'd never seen him in action.

It was . . . impressive.

But she'd have time to think about that later.

She took his hand, and he led her out of the parking garage. Once they emerged, they ran toward an SUV parked on the street.

He clicked the fob in his hand, and the lights blinked.

Shouts sounded behind them. Another spray of bullets targeted them.

The next moment, he shoved her inside and dove in after her.

CHAPTER
THREE

HUDSON STARTED the engine and sped down the road.

As he did, he glanced in his rearview mirror.

A gunman ran to the curb while firing more rounds at them.

People on the sidewalk screamed, fled.

As more bullets hit the SUV, he looked over at Teagan as she crouched low in her seat.

"Are you okay?" he asked.

"I . . . I think so."

He let out the breath he'd been holding.

Teagan.

His Teagan.

She was alive.

He had so many questions.

But he couldn't ask them right now.

He and Teagan weren't in the clear yet.

These guys were trained, experienced killers.

He needed to get her out of Dallas and to Arizona where she'd be safe. Where they could talk.

He jerked the wheel and made a sharp left turn, barely avoiding oncoming traffic.

"Hudson?" Fear laced her voice.

"I've got this, Teagan," he told her. "Just put your seatbelt on. And hold tight."

Teagan.

That was how he would refer to her, no matter what she said.

Because that's who she was. He was certain of it.

Even if it didn't make sense.

He took another sharp left.

Teagan gasped and closed her eyes. He only caught a brief glimpse of her reaction before turning his attention back to the road.

And just in time.

A car appeared behind him.

"Oh, no . . ." he muttered.

"Oh, no?" More anxiety laced her voice.

"Get down in your seat."

She bent forward, her hands over her head, and didn't ask any questions.

Just in time.

A bullet shattered the back window.

Teagan let out a soft scream, and her arms tightened over her head.

Hudson hated to hear her fear. Hated whatever she'd gone through up to this point.

The Farinos weren't to be messed with. They were

wrapped up in so many illegal activities that Hudson couldn't list them all. They also left a string of dead bodies wherever they went.

So how had Teagan ended up with them?

He'd ask those questions later.

First, he had to make sure they got out of this alive.

As the car approached his bumper, he knew that would be easier said than done.

***

Teagan felt the danger zinging through the air and knew her future was precarious at best right now.

Her heart thudded in her ears with each second that passed.

She glanced in the side mirror.

The car behind them closed in.

Then she felt a nudge.

Teagan's throat tightened.

If the Farinos caught her, she would literally be locked away where no one could find her. She'd lose any hope of freedom.

Then, once the family was done using her for their purposes, they'd kill her.

Teagan had no doubt about that.

A cry bubbled inside her at the thought.

She should have known better than to think she could escape.

But what other choice did she have?

Ricky was dead. She had no one to protect her anymore.

Yet the stakes were higher than ever.

The car rammed them, and she lurched into the dashboard.

She held back a cry and kept her hands over her head, expecting another hit.

Or worse.

"Oh, no, you don't," Hudson muttered.

Suddenly, they turned. Swerved. Drifted.

Horns honked. Tires screeched. The smell of burning rubber filled the air.

They were going to die.

Teagan was certain of it.

But she was also certain that Hudson was capable.

If anyone could get them out of this mess, he could.

He was the strongest, bravest man she'd ever known.

And he was here. With her now.

It seemed surreal.

Minutes seemed to stretch as Teagan waited for another nudge. Or a lurch. Or a crash.

Instead, they cruised down the road with no turns or sudden accelerations.

After a few more minutes, she raised her head slightly, expecting the worst but hoping for the best.

Was it possible they were out of danger?

Or was that just wishful thinking?

CHAPTER
FOUR

HUDSON GLANCED in the rearview mirror one more time.

It appeared he'd lost those guys.

But he wasn't sure for how long.

Right now, he needed to get as far away from them as possible.

Thankfully, he had a full tank of gas, five guns, and even some snacks.

He'd come prepared.

He was a former Navy SEAL. That's what they did.

"You can sit up now." He glanced at Teagan as she slouched down in her seat, her entire body tense with fear. "We lost them."

Slowly, she lifted her head.

She glanced around hesitantly as if in doubt.

Then she fully rose.

Scanned her surroundings again.

Finally, she let out a breath and leaned back in her

seat, a small semblance of relief softening her features. "I didn't think we were going to make it out of that one."

"Of course, we did. I'm not planning to lose this battle."

She glanced at him, her eyes orbs of emotion.

Eyes that had once mesmerized him.

Eyes Hudson had dreamed about seeing again . . . even if the reality of that hope was gut-wrenching.

"Are you okay?" He raised his voice to be heard over the roar of the wind through the broken back window.

Teagan ran a hand through her hair, and shards of glass tumbled to the rubber floor mats.

"I'm fine." Her voice trembled.

Hudson kept his gaze on everything around him. One moment of letting down his guard could end in destruction.

This hadn't worked out as he'd planned.

When he'd grabbed Teagan, he'd only had two minutes to get her to his SUV.

When he'd realized who she was, his plan had nearly been derailed.

That could have been a fatal mistake.

Teagan stared at Hudson.

Yes, Hudson.

The only man she'd ever loved.

He looked the same, only a little older. Had grief done that to him?

He had a sturdy, muscular build—but not in an overblown way. His hair was dark, and he had a slight beard that matched. His blue eyes were kind and had always been able to melt her insides in an instant.

She'd missed looking into them. Holding his strong hands. Feeling his warm embrace.

A cry caught in her throat at the thought.

She knew she couldn't deny the truth about who she really was. She'd slipped up and said Hudson's name before he introduced himself.

She was usually so careful. But seeing Hudson had left her feeling off-balance.

Even after everything that happened with Ricky, she'd never felt about her husband the way she had about Hudson.

Not even close.

Now Hudson was here sitting beside her. Taking her somewhere safe.

Protecting her.

She didn't know how long she'd be in this vehicle with him, but certainly long enough to talk. Suddenly, the sides of the vehicle felt like they were closing in.

Desperation pounded at her temples—desperation to get away.

Why couldn't anyone else besides Hudson have been sent to rescue her?

"We're going to need to find a motel for the night." Hudson stared at the road ahead as they left the city behind them. "But we'll get you to the ranch where you'll be safe. We just need to leave a breadcrumb trail first—one that leads away from our actual location."

Teagan licked her suddenly dry lips.

"Whatever you think is best." Her voice cracked.

She didn't even know where she was going.

A woman named Charlie had told her it was better if she didn't know. That the location was top secret, but that she would be safe there.

Teagan was trying to be compliant, even though everything inside her wanted answers.

She stole a glance at Hudson.

She'd expected him to ask questions. But he was surprisingly quiet. Probably stewing over his thoughts. Stewing over the fact she was still alive.

She glanced behind them again just to double-check that no one was following. The coast appeared to be clear, as the saying went.

She only hoped that assumption was correct.

She knew the Farinos. Knew how they operated.

They'd hunt her down with everything in their power. They wouldn't give up until they got what they wanted.

But if anyone could help her, it was Hudson. Strong and capable Hudson. He'd always been that way.

Teagan didn't say anything, and he didn't pressure her. She was thankful for that. But she knew she wouldn't be able to delay this conversation long.

Another hour passed with still hardly any words spoken between the two of them. Instead, Hudson had made a slew of phone calls as he updated his team-mates on what had happened.

Finally, Hudson pulled to a stop in front of an old motel in the middle of what appeared to be nowhere.

Teagan had noticed that Hudson had turned several times before stopping, no doubt trying to throw anyone following them off their trail. But she had no idea where she was right now.

Nor did she know how long she'd be able to avoid talking about the subject of how she was still alive.

Probably not long.

Thankfully, the two of them had other worries right now.

Worries like staying alive.

CHAPTER
FIVE

HUDSON PULLED into a parking space near the motel office, where a VACANCY sign blinked, the second C in the word blacked out.

It wasn't the classiest establishment, but it would work. At least, it was secluded with a large swath of woods stretching behind it.

Hudson had to use every ounce of self-control not to ask Teagan any questions on the drive here. But he had so many. He almost didn't know where to start.

He only knew he wanted to be able to look Teagan in the eye when they talked.

That was the primary reason he had busied himself with the phone calls on the drive here instead of pushing her.

That, and the fact that he needed to keep his eyes on the road, to look for anybody who might still be tailing them.

But he'd been careful. He'd made strategic turns.

From what he knew about the Farinos, they were good. Really good. Hudson knew that no matter what happened, he couldn't get too comfortable or feel too safe.

He directed Teagan to wait in the SUV as he ran inside to get a room.

It wouldn't take long to pay and grab the key. Teagan would be okay in the SUV by herself for a couple of minutes.

After Hudson checked in, he drove to the backside of the motel and parked. He couldn't chance someone recognizing his SUV.

This wasn't his first rodeo.

In fact, this was his eighth extraction in the past year. Each one had different challenges. Each had been successful.

Several minutes later, he and Teagan were settled into an old motel room that probably hadn't been updated in three decades. Dark paneling lined the walls. An old boxy television sat on the dresser. The bathroom had cracked tiled floors and a dingy bathtub coated with . . . something he didn't want to know.

But it would be a place to sleep for the night.

He left Teagan in the room long enough to grab a few things from the SUV—including some snacks and drinks. He set them on the dresser in case she needed something.

With the doors locked and curtains drawn, he sat down and glanced at Teagan.

He still couldn't believe she was in front of him.

And still beautiful, even with the new hair color.

He'd known her as a brunette with wavy hair that came down well below her shoulders. She had brown eyes—intelligent eyes—and almost quirky movements. He'd found them adorable. Her brisk steps and the animated way she talked with her hands. The way her expression could never hide exactly what she was thinking.

He'd mourned that woman.

Yet now here she was.

Like an impossible dream come true.

"Where are we?" She sat cross-legged on the bed as she waited for his answer.

"Near the Arkansas border."

Her eyebrows shot up. "Arkansas?"

"It's a misdirection. I didn't want to let Farino's guys know where we're really going, just to be safe. So, I went the opposite way for now instead."

Teagan nodded slowly before rubbing her throat. Her gaze jerked up to meet his, hesitation—and maybe some fear—there. "I'm sure you have a lot of questions."

"That would be an understatement." But, even in his frustration, he hated her fear. Certainly, she didn't fear him, right? He'd never laid a hand on her—or any woman, for that matter.

She nodded slowly again. "I figured as much. I—"

She abruptly stopped, looked down, and her hand went to her stomach as if pain coursed through her.

Concern rushed through him, and he quickly moved beside her. "What's wrong?"

Before Teagan could answer, she rose from the bed and rushed into the bathroom before throwing up.

As much as Hudson didn't want to feel compassion toward her, he did. He had the urge to check on her. To hold her hair out of the way. To tell her everything would be okay.

But he didn't. It was too soon. Things had happened too fast.

She'd always had a nervous stomach, and clearly the stress from today was getting to her.

Finally, she returned to the room, her skin flushed as she sat on the edge of the bed.

"You okay?" he asked.

She nodded. "I'm better."

"Good." Now it was time to get some answers.

No more beating around the proverbial bush.

He had to know how she was still alive . . . and why she'd put him through a living nightmare.

———

Teagan rubbed her hands on her jeans. She'd dressed in flats and a black tank top for a day of shopping. If she'd known the turns today would take, she would have chosen something more sensible.

Her throat burned from throwing up, and her stomach still felt queasy. She grabbed the package of crackers that Hudson had set out and opened it, the crinkling sound of the wrapper twisting her nerves even tighter.

Slowly, she nibbled on the peanut butter cracker, praying her stomach would settle.

The last thing she wanted was to throw up in front of Hudson again.

He sat across from her, on the opposite bed, a patient expression on his face.

He'd always been so patient. So kind.

That made the events of the past two years even more heartbreaking.

She'd always loved him. All this time she'd never stopped.

"I'm sorry." Her voice cracked as she said the words.

Hudson stared at her, and Teagan knew he wasn't sure if she was sorry about throwing up or sorry about what she'd done to him.

She supposed, in a strange way, it was both.

She rubbed her hands on her jeans again, suddenly feeling clammy. "I never meant for any of this to happen. I never meant for you to see me again. I was supposed to disappear."

"Why?" He stared at her, years of hurt embedded in his gaze. "Why would you want to disappear?"

Nausea began to gurgle up again, but she held it back. Not now. She couldn't avoid this conversation any longer.

"I know this is going to be a lot, and that it will sound unbelievable," she started. "But what I'm about to say is the truth."

Hudson waited, still not saying anything.

Teagan cleared her throat before diving in. "I was told if I didn't leave, you would be killed."

She pressed the back of her hand against her mouth, fighting more nausea.

This time, the gut-wrenching memories caused the feeling.

A knot formed between Hudson's eyes as if he hadn't heard her correctly. "Who would kill me?"

"The Farinos."

He blinked as if he still wasn't comprehending what she said. "What do you mean? Why would the Farinos want to kill me? I've never even had any encounters with them."

"You haven't, but I have." More memories battered her. "I dated their son, Ricky, before I dated you."

Hudson blinked again. "He's the guy you broke up with before moving to San Diego?"

She nodded. "He didn't take our breakup well."

"I'm still not tracking where you're going with this . . ."

She pressed her eyes shut. "I didn't want to go with them. Didn't want to get back with Ricky. But before my trip to Brazil, they cornered me. They told me I had to go with them or that you'd die. Then they showed me a picture of you with a gun's laser sight on your back."

"Why would they threaten me?"

She rubbed her cheek, feeling the strain on her expression. "Ricky—their only child—had been suicidal since we broke up. They knew I wasn't going to go with them willingly. So, they manipulated the situation."

"So, you faked your death?"

"*They* faked my death. I had no idea what they'd done until I saw something about it on the news later. I had no choice but to go along with their plan or else . . ."

You would die.

She didn't say the words, but she knew Hudson understood.

Teagan gave him a moment to comprehend what she'd told him.

It was a lot. It was still a lot, even for her.

She waited quietly as he collected his thoughts.

Each moment that went by seemed an eternity.

HUDSON COULDN'T BELIEVE what he'd just heard.

He had no reason to think Teagan was lying . . . other than the fact he'd been deceived two years ago.

Had someone really gone as far as to use his life to exploit Teagan?

And if that was the truth . . . he could hardly even comprehend it. His heart twisted into knots at the thought.

These past two years . . . he and Teagan could have been together? He could have avoided the all-consuming grief. His sleepless nights. His trips to the therapist.

Instead, someone had forced her to disappear. To change her identity. To leave him behind.

His heart twisted tighter.

"I don't know what to say." Then another thought hit him. "Did they force you to get married?"

He'd read the file for this assignment. He'd seen what it said about Teagan and her new identity.

How did *that* fit in with her story?

Teagan averted her gaze to her hands. "Getting married and being compliant was the only way to survive. In my heart, my marriage wasn't real."

"You never tried to get away?" He was trying to process this. But it seemed so extreme.

"They gave me a new name. They wanted me to be dead because they knew otherwise you'd come looking for me." She paused and rubbed her throat. "I did try to run once."

"And?"

She pulled down her shirt collar. "This happened when I was caught."

He sucked in a breath when he saw the scar there. It was long—probably three inches—and jagged.

And entirely too close to her heart.

"Teagan . . ."

She shrugged. "Eventually, I just resigned myself to my fate. I lost all hope."

Hudson swallowed hard, trying to find the right words. "I'm sorry, Teagan."

"After Ricky died, I knew things would get worse, that the Farinos would have no reason to keep me around. When I had the opportunity to run again, I knew it was worth it."

"Ricky died?" Hudson knew what happened, but he wanted to hear the details from Teagan's perspective.

She nodded. "We buried him three months ago. But

I never loved him. I know that sounds harsh. But it's true."

Hudson continued to study Teagan. He didn't see any signs of deceit on her expression. Still, this all sounded so outlandish.

But what if her story was true?

Had the Farinos really used Teagan to placate Ricky? It sounded like they thought of her as a possession instead of a human capable of making her own decisions.

If that really was the case, then his heart broke for her.

Hudson tried to figure out what he wanted to ask next as questions spun in his mind.

Before he could, headlights flashed in the window.

Someone had just pulled into the motel.

He rose.

Hudson had to make sure it wasn't one of the men who'd been chasing them earlier.

A moment of panic raced through Teagan.

Was it even possible that these guys had somehow found them here?

She didn't think so.

Unless there was some way they were being tracked.

She reached for the gold pendant at her throat and sucked in a breath as she remembered when Frank

Farino had given it to her, when he'd insisted she always wear it to show she was part of this family.

Was it . . . ?

She swallowed hard, her thoughts racing.

She watched as Hudson peeked from the corner of the window, careful to stay out of sight.

The way his body went rigid confirmed something was wrong.

"Hudson?" Her voice trembled as she said the words.

He didn't say anything. Instead, he just watched, his body still.

"You're scaring me," she whispered. "Is it them?"

Hudson suddenly turned to her. "Teagan, we need to move."

Her heart beat harder.

She'd hoped she was wrong. That all her assumptions were incorrect.

But it appeared they weren't.

Farino's men had found them.

"What are we going to do?" Her voice trembled as she asked the question.

"We've got to get out of here." Hudson's neck and jaw stiffened. "They're going to start checking all of these rooms. We don't have much time."

He grabbed her hand and pulled her in the bathroom.

Working quickly, he climbed on the toilet and opened a window above it.

"We can fit through this," he said. "I'm going to lift you up."

"But . . ." Teagan had felt fear before in her life. Many times.

For some reason, the feeling felt greater now than ever before.

"You can do this," Hudson murmured. "I'm going to be right behind you. I promise."

Somewhere in the distance, she heard a door bust open.

These guys were going room to room looking for them, weren't they?

She had no idea how they were going to get out of this situation. All she could do right now was trust Hudson. She had no other choice.

He boosted her up, and she scrambled through the window, catching herself before dropping to the other side.

She didn't fear getting hurt as much as she feared calling attention to what they were doing.

Once she found her balance, she took a few steps back, out of Hudson's way, and glanced at the darkness around her.

Everything appeared clear.

Hudson landed beside her with the prowess of a cat.

He glanced around also before taking her hand again. "Come on. We need to get to the SUV."

"Won't they see us when we drive away? Certainly, they'll catch up with us."

Teagan knew by his expression that she was right, and that Hudson was thinking the same thing.

"I'll figure something out," he told her. "You're just going to have to trust me."

She'd always trusted Hudson. It was easy to do.

But she hadn't been in this type of situation with him before.

Had never put her life in his hands.

She'd never thought she'd have to.

CHAPTER
SEVEN

HUDSON GLANCED around for something that could help him.

He didn't have much time to figure this out, but he could do this. He had no other choice.

He had to distract those men somehow.

Then he spotted his solution.

He grabbed a cement block lying behind the building.

This could work.

"Stay with me," he said to Teagan as he darted toward the SUV.

He opened the driver's side door and placed the block on the floorboard.

Working quickly, he put the vehicle in Neutral and began pushing it to the side of the building.

Teagan ran behind the SUV and pushed also.

He did his best to stabilize the wheel so the vehicle wouldn't veer all over the parking lot.

He hoped this worked. But a lot of things needed to fall in place for that to be the case.

When in position, he motioned for Teagan to back away. Once she was at a safe distance, he lifted up a quick prayer and started the SUV.

He knew those men would hear the engine, and he and Teagan wouldn't have much time to get away after that happened.

But this could work. It had to work.

Thankfully, the darkness would work in their favor. These guys shouldn't be able to see that no one was inside the vehicle.

Just as he was about to put the SUV into Drive, Teagan tossed something inside.

The gold pendant necklace she'd been wearing landed on the passenger seat.

There must be a tracker on it, he realized. It was the only thing that made sense.

After all, these guys had found them somehow, and Hudson had been careful to cover his tracks.

He was glad Teagan had thought to get rid of it.

Hudson lifted another prayer before wedging the cement block against the accelerator and putting the vehicle in Drive.

Then he watched as the SUV zoomed from behind the building and down the street, the driver's side door swinging shut with the momentum.

So far so good.

But he knew he didn't have much time to make his next move.

Teagan watched the SUV speed away, disbelief stretching through her.

She might take a moment to reflect on how brilliant Hudson's plan was. But she didn't have time for that.

Hudson grabbed her hand again and pulled her into the woods. There wasn't anything romantic about the way he gripped her, tugging her along.

But she still felt comforted by his touch.

Moving as quickly as possible, they raced between the trees and into the darkness.

Teagan didn't dare look back. She had to keep an eye on where they were headed.

As soon as those guys figured out the SUV was empty, they'd come back here to track Hudson and Teagan down.

And, when that happened, Farino's men would be relentless. They'd keep searching until they found Hudson and Teagan.

The first part of Hudson's plan seemed brilliant. But Teagan wasn't sure how this next part would play out.

After they'd run for probably fifteen minutes, Hudson slowed a little, released her hand, and grabbed his phone. He dialed, spoke to someone in low tones.

Teagan couldn't make out what was being said.

It didn't matter.

At least they had service.

Long after the conversation ended, they kept going.

Finally, Hudson stopped and pulled her behind a

tree. He put a finger to his lips to indicate for her to wait.

Teagan took a moment to catch her breath.

Then she listened.

Were those guys coming after them yet? Did they have enough of a head start to lose them?

She wasn't sure.

"I have a plan," Hudson whispered. "But we're going to need to kill some time."

Her eyebrows shot up.

Kill some time?

That seemed risky.

Especially considering someone was trying to kill them.

CHAPTER
EIGHT

HUDSON PRAYED HIS PLAN WORKED. The strategy was tricky, but it was the only option he could think of considering their current circumstances.

He and Teagan couldn't afford to stay in the same place for too long. He knew that.

Surely by now those men had discovered the SUV was just a ruse. They'd probably gone back to the motel and searched all the rooms again.

The only logical place for them to search next were these woods.

Hudson had examined a map before he started this mission. He knew that this forest was extensive. He also knew there were several clearings.

That's where he and Teagan needed to head.

Although it seemed counterintuitive because they'd be out in the open, the wide-open space was necessary for the next part of his plan.

Until then, they needed to stay clear of those men.

Just as the thought went through Hudson's head, a stick cracked in the distance.

His breath caught.

It was Farino's men. Hudson was certain of it.

The guys were trying to be stealthy as they walked through the dark woods searching for him and Teagan.

But Hudson had been trained to be stealthy.

Hudson gripped Teagan's hand, meeting her gaze with a meaningful look.

She nodded as if she would follow him anywhere.

Good. Because he had to keep her safe.

Not only because she was the woman he'd once loved.

But also because he had more questions for her.

The darkness helped hide them as they wandered the woods.

As they moved, Hudson prayed his plan worked.

Especially since everything was on the line.

Things couldn't have gotten more off track though.

He had known this assignment wouldn't be easy. But he'd never anticipated all this.

"Hudson?" Teagan's voice sounded just above a whisper.

Before he could respond, another stick snapped. Closer this time.

The guys were closing in.

And it was too late to run.

Their best chance was to simply hide. These guys didn't have dogs to trace their scent, and, hopefully, they wouldn't be able to locate them. The nighttime would serve as their friend.

He led her to a rock formation not far away.

They could tuck themselves beneath it and stay out of sight.

At least, he prayed that was the case.

They reached it just in time.

He heard someone muttering as if on the phone.

"We're close," the man said. "I can feel it."

He wasn't wrong.

Hudson nudged Teagan, indicating for her to wedge into the space below the boulder.

They would blend in with the inky shadows there. It was their best chance.

This situation reminded him of a mission he'd once been on in Afghanistan. The terrorists had been hot on his team's trail.

The nighttime had been the only thing to save them. Thankfully, those guys hadn't had night vision goggles.

He didn't think these guys did either.

Even if they'd been keeping an eye on Teagan, certainly they hadn't anticipated all this.

At his direction, Teagan pressed herself beneath the small rock overhang. Hudson squeezed in beside her. His all-black clothing would help conceal them.

But as he lay so close, Teagan's rapid heartbeat thumped against his arm.

She was scared, and rightfully so.

Hudson closed his eyes and prayed they'd remain out of sight and safe.

They had too much unfinished business between them for things to end right now.

CHAPTER
NINE

TEAGAN ALMOST COULDN'T HANDLE BEING SO close to Hudson.

She'd dreamed about this for so long. Dreamed about what life might have been like with him by her side.

Then she'd had to let those dreams die. They were too painful.

She'd had to regroup. She'd forced herself to put those memories aside. To let any hope she had inside die.

It was the only way she'd been able to survive.

As she pressed herself farther into the darkness between the rock and the ground, she heard movement.

Footsteps sounded. Leaves crunched. A conversation drifted.

She heard one of the men mutter that they were close.

Teagan thought she and Hudson were blending into the shadows right now. But she couldn't be certain.

She stared at the rock above her for only a moment before turning her head. When she did, she saw Hudson studying her.

Their faces were so close that she sucked in a breath.

He was still so handsome.

What she wouldn't do to be able to run her fingers across his jaw.

But that opportunity had died right along with Teagan Murphy.

She'd been forced to transform into Katerina Farino. They didn't want anyone to look for her, to get suspicious.

But the name had never felt right to her.

Then again, she'd learned to do whatever she needed to survive.

Something buzzed next to her.

Hudson's phone, she realized.

Slowly, he took it from his pocket and held it close to conceal the light.

He grunted as he glanced at the screen.

"Hudson?" she whispered.

He shook his head and shoved the phone back into his pocket.

Just as one of the men walked directly beside them . . . the beam of the man's flashlight bouncing dangerously close to their location.

Their ride was here. Early.

That's what the text had said.

Hudson knew he and Teagan didn't have much time before these guys figured out what was going on.

He couldn't chance that.

That meant he and Teagan needed to move. Soon.

For now, Hudson remained frozen in place.

Black boots paced beside him, and a flashlight beam skittered around the area.

But the man didn't see them.

Then another set of legs appeared.

The two men chasing them had paused beside the rock where Hudson and Teagan hid.

Clearly, they were trying to regroup.

But one wrong move on Hudson's or Teagan's end, and everything would fall apart.

"Where did they go?" one of the men asked.

"I don't know. They have to be around here somewhere."

"There's no way they got away. We'll search this entire forest if that's what we have to do."

"You know we do. If Frank finds out that we let Kat get away, we're both dead. It won't be a bullet in the brain. He'll put us in a pit and leave us there to die a long, slow, painful death. Just like he did to those other guys who failed."

Hudson's heart beat harder.

He'd been around some ruthless people before. Some of the most evil and vile men in the world, for that matter.

But he knew Frank Farino was right up there with the worst of them.

The man had a lot of blood on his hands. But he was smart enough to cover his crimes so that none of them directly led back to him. Still, anyone with any knowledge of law enforcement and crime had heard about the family's atrocities.

Hudson willed himself not to make any noise.

But a mental clock ticked in his head.

He and Teagan had to get out of here.

Backup would arrive in ten minutes. If his estimate was right, ten minutes was about how long it would take to get to the location where they'd be extracted.

They had to be there waiting, or it would be too late.

He glanced over and saw the two men still standing there. Not moving.

That's when he knew he and Teagan weren't out of the woods yet.

CHAPTER
TEN

TEAGAN DIDN'T KNOW what was happening.

She only knew danger was close.

What if these guys didn't leave? What if they waited them out? What would she and Hudson do then?

Her heart felt lodged in her throat, and her lungs tight. Every part of her wanted to run. To scream. To do anything to get away from these guys.

Instead, she needed to try to make herself disappear.

Disappearing had been her plan from the start—disappearing from the Farinos.

Against her will, Teagan had started a new life once. She should be able to do it again.

This time would be more complicated—but at least she would be free.

Finally, one of the men spoke again. "Let's split up. You go that way, and I'll go this way. Call out if you see them."

"Okay. But if not, we meet back here in twenty. Got it?"

"Got it."

She didn't recognize their voices. They could be any one of Farino's henchmen. He had more than she could count. She hadn't met them all. But they all had one thing in common.

They were all well-paid and ruthless.

Hudson turned to her and whispered, "We've got to get out of here, and we don't have much time. Follow me. Be as quiet as possible."

Tension buzzed in her ears.

Just what was his plan?

She didn't know. She only knew she had to trust him, and she had to move.

Now.

Hudson rolled out from beneath the rocks before helping Teagan out.

He scanned the area around them.

The gunmen were gone. For now.

But he and Teagan didn't have any time to waste.

He grabbed her hand again. "Let's go."

He knew that at any moment now, a new sound would fill the air and draw attention.

They had to make it to the clearing before that happened.

His heart pounded harder. Adrenaline had helped

him on his missions before. He needed to use that epinephrine to his advantage right now as well.

He moved quickly but carefully as he pulled Teagan behind him, heading toward the extraction point. Their footsteps gently padded the ground. Any sound could give away their location.

They'd walked five minutes when he heard it.

The sound of chopper blades.

Their ride.

Ghost had gotten here much sooner than Hudson had anticipated.

It was too late to try to be quiet now.

"Run!" he said as he took off into a sprint, still holding Teagan's hand.

He and Teagan emerged from the woods in time to see the copter landing in an open expanse.

Teagan glanced at Hudson. "You have access to a helicopter?"

"I've got resources at my disposal. Besides, desperate times call for desperate measures."

But as soon as he said the words, gunfire filled the air.

Those guys had found them.

And they were shooting.

HUDSON'S backup plan was better than Teagan had imagined.

Now the trick would be getting to the copter before they were shot.

As the thought raced through her head, another bullet pierced the air.

Instinctively, she ducked.

Hudson kept pulling her forward, breaking away from the protection the woods had provided.

Nothing but an open field stood between them and the copter.

Getting there would be risky.

But they had no other options.

Hudson kept a firm grip on her arm as they continued toward the copter.

The door opened, and a man motioned them forward.

More gunfire filled the air. Shouts sounded from behind them.

Teagan swallowed back a scream.

They hadn't come this far to die now.

They could do this.

Adrenaline seemed to pump through Hudson, and he didn't slow down—not until they reached the helicopter.

As soon as they were close enough, the man inside grabbed her and lifted her inside so quickly she felt as weightless as a ragdoll.

Then Hudson climbed in, and the copter lifted into the air.

Teagan's hands trembled as she slid into a seat and tried to snap her seatbelt in place. She couldn't seem to line up the mechanism.

Hudson reached over, his hands steady as he latched it for her.

Teagan's heart simultaneously seemed to pound harder at his touch and calm down knowing he was nearby.

She wasn't sure which was accurate, but they both felt true at this moment.

Hudson handed her a headset, and she slipped it on just as the pilot said, "Hold on. This might be a rocky ride."

As he said the words, more bullets peppered the air.

Teagan ducked as one clinked against the metal exterior of the helicopter.

They'd been hit, she realized.

Would they crash? Would this all be over now?

The man who'd helped her aboard opened the door, drew his gun, and fired back.

Teagan closed her eyes and prayed she'd have a happy ending to this escape.

Hudson pulled on his own headset and watched as Jesse Marx aimed his gun and shot toward the men on the ground.

His bullets held off the other guys long enough for the chopper to get in the air.

But he'd heard a bullet hit the copter, and he hoped the shot didn't take them down.

"Ghost?" He glanced at the pilot in the front seat.

His jaw hardened. "We're good. We just need to get out of here."

The copter lifted higher before swooping into the night.

Bullets still sounded, but none of them reached them.

"Will these guys be able to trace the copter's tail number?" Hudson asked.

"Let's hope not," Ghost said.

"We need to get somewhere safe, just in case." Hudson didn't like the idea of those men going after Ghost.

"Let me worry about that. You just worry about keeping Ms. Farino safe."

No, not Ms. Farino. *Teagan*.

But Hudson didn't say that aloud.

He glanced at Teagan and noted how pale her face looked as she gripped the armrest and stared out the window.

"We're okay," he reassured her.

Wrinkles formed at the corner of her eyes as she nodded, her face nearly stoic with fear. "I hope so."

"Kat." He decided to use the name everyone else knew. For now, at least. "These are my colleagues. Nate Casper here is the pilot, but he goes by Ghost."

He pointed at Ghost, who raised a hand in the air and saluted.

"And this is Jesse Marx. They were waiting nearby as backup just in case things went south. It's a good thing they were."

A faint smile brushed her lips before quickly disappearing. "Thank you all. I feel terrible I'm putting you through all this trouble."

"It's what we do," Jesse said. "No need for apologies."

The team at Vanishing Ranch didn't charge for their extractions. Their only concern was helping those who couldn't help themselves—by giving them a chance for a new life. That was what their leader, Charlie Soldier, always said.

Teagan glanced over at him, questions in her gaze as they soared into the night. "What now?"

He heard the fear in her voice. She knew they weren't out of danger yet.

These guys would keep searching for her.

"Now, you just take it easy," he finally said. She'd been through enough for one day. "We're going to get you to safety. Then we're going to make sure these guys never find you again."

The lines around Teagan's eyes seemed to soften. But only for a moment. Then the tension returned.

She didn't believe that would be the case, did she?

Hudson remembered the jagged scar she'd shown him.

What else had the Farinos done to her?

He didn't know, but he had to make sure they never got ahold of Teagan again.

TWELVE

TEAGAN AWOKE with a start and glanced around in panic.

Where was she?

Her mother-in law, Lucia Farino, had threatened if Teagan tried to leave a second time that she would lock her in a room where she would never see daylight again.

Teagan had no doubt the woman was telling the truth, considering what had happened the first time she'd tried to escape.

But Teagan wasn't locked away in a room right now.

She was surrounded by windows.

And movement.

She was in a car, she realized.

She glanced beside her and saw Hudson there.

Yes, Hudson.

He hadn't been a dream.

He offered a soft smile when he saw she was awake.

"Good morning."

She blinked several times, trying to recall how she'd gotten here.

That's right. The helicopter. They'd flown for a few hours before landing.

Then they transferred to a vehicle.

It had all been so dark when it happened. She must have rested her head against the window and fallen asleep.

As she glanced around again, she realized it was daylight outside.

She'd slept harder than she thought.

But it was better that way. She'd been so tired and stressed lately. Her body needed to rest.

"Where are we?" Her voice sounded raspy with sleep.

"We're here." He nodded in front of them toward a Western-style iron-and-wood gate with the letters VR stretched across the top.

"VR?"

"Vanishing Ranch. You woke up just in time."

She sat up straighter and glanced in the front seat where Jesse sat behind the wheel.

Wow, everything really was a blur.

Had Hudson not slept at all? It didn't appear so. He looked as alert as ever, though, with no signs of drowsiness.

As her mental cobwebs cleared, the name sank in. *Vanishing Ranch.*

How appropriate.

"We'll get you inside," Hudson said. "You can settle down and maybe get a shower and rest a bit. Then we can show you around."

"As much as I'd love a shower, I don't have any clothes to change into."

"We have everything you need. No worries."

Teagan nodded, wishing she felt at peace. She didn't.

The emotion seemed premature.

They pulled through the gate. Teagan glanced back and watched as the arms closed behind them, ironclad as if no one else would ever be allowed inside.

Good. She hoped that really was the case.

As she glanced through the windshield, she sucked in a breath when the ranch came into view, complete with Western-styled buildings, a stable, and even an old stagecoach.

She felt as if she was entering another world.

This was going to be interesting . . . to say the least.

Hudson left Sienna Fleming, one of his colleagues, posted outside Teagan's cabana as she got settled. Not that she needed protection here. They were miles and miles from everything.

But she might have questions. He felt better knowing someone was close.

There were eight cabanas located on the property, and that's where their guests stayed as well as certain members of management. These accommodations were more private than the bunkhouse where the rest of the staff slept.

Teagan would be fine for the time being.

Right now, Hudson needed to talk to Charlie.

He strode into the mess hall and headed toward the offices located on the far side of the space.

He knocked on her partly closed door and waited until she called, "Come in."

He stepped inside and spotted Charlie. The woman was fascinating, to say the least. She had dark hair and loved her leather jackets—unless it was a hundred degrees outside.

She was confident, and everyone around her knew it. She'd commanded the respect of former warriors, and she hadn't let anyone down yet.

She was part CEO, part cowgirl, and part someone you wanted to kick back with and watch a football game.

Her righthand man, Monroe, stood beside her, with his linebacker build and protective stance.

"I heard you had a close call." Charlie leaned back in her chair, looking as easygoing as ever—even though a tiger lurked inside her, lunging if provoked. Thankfully, that didn't happen very often.

"You can say that again." Hudson sat across from her. "But we came through."

"You always do." She stared at him, tilting her head. "But I have a feeling there's more you want to talk about."

"That's a good guess." He shifted in his seat, wondering how to word his next statement. He decided to be blunt. "Did you know Kat Farino is actually Teagan Murphy?"

Surprise lit Charlie's eyes. "Teagan Murphy?"

"My fiancée. Who supposedly died two years ago."

Charlie's eyebrows shot up. "What?"

Hudson nodded. Then he filled her in on what Teagan had told him.

Her eyes widened more with each new detail, and she appeared to be earnestly surprised.

She hadn't known Kat Farino was actually Teagan Murphy. If what Teagan had told him was true, no one knew except the Farinos. Teagan had practically been locked away as a hostage for the past two years —a hostage with a spending account. But she'd still been a hostage, someone who would be punished if she ran.

"This is certainly an interesting turn of events." Charlie tapped her fingers together in front of her.

"Interesting. Shocking. Almost unbelievable."

"You didn't know she'd dated a Farino?" Charlie narrowed her eyes as she waited for his answer.

"All Teagan told me was that she'd dated someone who was possessive and who'd gotten wrapped up in some trouble. She'd taken a new job in San Diego to get away from him. But she never mentioned him giving her trouble, and she never went into any details about what happened. She said she wanted to put the past behind her."

"Are you okay with all this?" Charlie eyed him closely. "Okay with Teagan being here?"

"Of course." He was a professional after all. He could keep his past from interfering with his work.

Besides, he wouldn't trust anyone else with Teagan. Not that his teammates weren't trustworthy. But he and Teagan had too much history between them.

He wanted to watch over her himself.

"At least, she can know she'll be safe here," Charlie said.

Hudson nodded, praying that was the case. But it almost seemed too easy, especially when he considered just how aggressive Farino's guys were.

A shadow filled the doorway, and Hudson turned to see Ghost standing there. A frown tugged at his lips.

"What's going on?" Charlie asked.

"I just got a call from a friend with the FAA," he said. "Someone is demanding information about all the flights in and out of Dallas last night—at all the airports, not just the major ones."

"You said you didn't have to file a flight plan, right?" Charlie asked.

"That's right. I covered my tracks." Ghost shifted. "My only worry is about who these guys have in their pockets. If they keep pushing, they could potentially find out information. Even if they do, it should only lead back to me. Not to this ranch. But I just wanted to give you the update."

Hudson swallowed, his throat suddenly tight.

This wasn't going to be as easy as he'd hoped.

CHAPTER
THIRTEEN

AS TEAGAN TOWEL dried her hair, she glanced in the mirror and hardly recognized the person she saw there.

Even after a couple of years of pretending to be someone she wasn't, her new identity had never felt real. Now, she'd have to do it all over again.

Take on a new name. Make up a new history. Make new friends and find a new community.

She'd done so before under duress.

During the first several months after she'd been abducted, she hadn't even been able to leave the compound. Eventually, the Farinos had allowed her small freedoms. But wherever she went, the Farinos sent their men with her to make sure she didn't try anything.

Just like when she went shopping yesterday.

She'd had to request the outing. Frank had approved it, as long as four guards accompanied her.

She knew the guards weren't there to keep her safe. Frank Farino wanted to make sure Teagan didn't try to run again. Make sure none of the family's enemies tried to hurt her—not because the Farinos cared about her.

Because they cared about their family name.

If Teagan died, they wanted to be the ones to make it happen.

All Teagan had ever really wanted to do was to settle down and have a family. A nice stable life. One like she'd had before her father died when she was a preteen. Before her mom had died of cancer when Teagan was in college.

She ambled to the dresser and found some of the clothes Hudson had said were waiting for her there. Sure enough, they were all her size.

She grabbed some jean shorts and a pink T-shirt and took them into the bathroom to change. Just as she slipped the shorts on, she paused at her reflection one more time.

She reached up, and her fingers skimmed her cheeks, still flushed from the warm shower.

She hated her long blonde hair. But Ricky had always liked blondes. Blondes with slender bodies and heavy eye makeup.

That look fit the family's style better.

They'd slowly transformed her into someone she wasn't.

It felt good not to wear any makeup or jewelry. To not feel the urge to dress to impress.

Could she really be safe here? Or was that too good to be true?

She wanted to believe that she could relax. But she hadn't relaxed in years.

She prayed she'd be safe. But at what cost would that come? Was she putting others in danger by being here?

That was the real question she needed to ask herself.

As the thought echoed in her head, her hands went to her stomach.

She pressed her fingers there and remembered the life growing inside her.

No one was supposed to know she was pregnant.

Yet she knew Lucia Farino had somehow figured it out. Teagan didn't know how, but she was certain that was the only reason the Farinos refused to let her go.

Lucia was even more cruel than Frank, though the woman covered it better. She could act accepting and kind—but she'd be the first to stab you in the back.

Teagan still remembered when the woman had cornered her at the compound right after she'd been brought there.

"My Ricky hasn't been the same since you broke up," she'd hissed.

Teagan had felt the desperate need to retreat from her, to get far away. But there was nowhere to go in the small room.

"I'm sorry," she'd whispered instead. *"I didn't intend to hurt him."*

Lucia had glared at her as if Teagan had purposefully hurt her son. "But you did! And now you need to make it right."

"But I don't love him. I love Hudson."

Lucia paced closer until she was in Teagan's face. "I never want to hear those words leave your mouth again. Your past with Hudson? It's over. He thinks you're dead. And we intend to keep it that way. Believe me when I tell you that you will regret it if you ever try to leave. My Ricky's happiness is my first and only priority."

"What are you saying?"

Lucia had straightened. "I'm saying the two of you need to talk. You need to let Ricky know you still care about him."

"That I care about him enough to leave my life behind and change my name?" The words had sounded audacious.

"You need to make it believable." Lucia practically spit out the words, the trademark cruel look in her otherwise frozen gaze. Uncountable plastic surgeries had practically erased any expression from her face. "Tell him you came here to make things right. That you changed your name because Hudson wouldn't let you go so you had no other choice."

Terror ripped through her at the thought. "You think Ricky will believe that?"

"He's attempted to kill himself twice. We've tried everything. You're the only one who can pull him out of this funk."

But could she? What if it didn't work?

Would they kill her?

Teagan knew the answer.

It was a most definite yes.

Now, they wanted to keep Ricky's baby.

That was exactly why Teagan needed to escape.

But she hadn't told Charlie or anyone else here at Vanishing Ranch about her condition.

That meant that Hudson didn't know either.

How would he react if he found out?

She closed her eyes and lifted another prayer for the growing life inside her.

Teagan hadn't been brave enough to go to the doctor yet. To get an ultrasound. But she was at least four months pregnant.

And there was no way she was letting her child get wrapped up with the Farino family.

Her jaw hardened.

She'd never allow it.

The only way they'd get their hands on her baby was over her dead body . . . literally.

Hudson dismissed Sienna before knocking on Teagan's door.

He sucked in a breath when she opened it.

Something about seeing her with her hair wet, no makeup, and wearing such casual clothing made her seem so vulnerable.

But was her clothing truly what caused the change or was there more to it? Something about her disposition seemed softer . . . it almost seemed to glow.

He pulled himself together when he realized he was staring. "As soon as you're ready, Charlie would like to meet with you."

She nodded. "I figured as much. I'm ready now."

"Come on then, and I'll show you to her office."

They slowly walked beside each other across the dusty ground. In the distance, he spotted Jesse and Sienna near the mess hall. They leaned close to each other and laughed about something before stealing a quick kiss.

The two were clearly in love.

"They're together?" Teagan asked.

He shrugged. "They're married . . . kind of."

"Kind of?"

"It's a really long story."

"Sounds like it." Teagan glanced around. "This is quite the place."

"I think so too. I wasn't sure exactly how much I'd like this place. It's not Montana. But I've grown to love it here."

"That doesn't surprise me. You've always loved horses and ranch life. It fits you."

Something about her approval brought him a burst of unwanted pleasure. She'd always understood him, always wanted him to be happy. She'd never been one of those women who'd tried to make him into someone he wasn't.

Finding someone like that had been a gift.

"When did you get out of the military?" Teagan asked.

Hudson forced his thoughts to jump back to the present. "A little over a year ago. I worked for a government contractor for a couple of months, but I hated being stuck in an office all day. That's when I started looking into other options, and Charlie recruited me to come here. I haven't looked back since then."

"The isolation doesn't bother you?"

"Not with all the land surrounding us. I feel like I can breathe here. Charlie owns two hundred acres. A national forest backs up against one side and miles of desert surround the other three. People just don't come out here on purpose, which makes it the perfect location to do what we need to do."

"I'm glad to hear that."

Hudson opened the door for Teagan and led her inside the mess hall, a place that had been decked out to look like an old Western saloon. The floors were dark wood, white ceiling tiles graced the space above them, a large mirror stretched across the back wall. Thick tables and hardy chairs dotted the space.

At one time, this place had been a dude ranch where guests had paid money to come for the full Western experience. Charlie had kept a lot of the decorations, probably because she had other things to spend money on. But somehow, the décor seemed to still fit the place.

Hudson led Teagan into the conference room where Charlie waited.

They needed to come up with a plan.

As much as he'd like to pretend that none of this ever happened and that Teagan could stay here forever, he knew that wasn't the case.

The Farinos wouldn't let her go without a fight, and they had all the resources in the world at their disposal.

TEAGAN'S NERVES BUZZED. "Wait . . . Charlie Soldier?"

Hudson nodded. "You've heard of her?"

"Who hasn't? I didn't realize that was the Charlie I was talking to."

"That's on purpose. She doesn't want everyone to know."

Charlie was the daughter of Benjamin Soldier, a former professional football player who'd given up his career to join the military and fight overseas. Unfortunately, he'd been killed during a battle. But his memory lived on, and he was still to this day honored as a hero by so many.

Charlie had been an ambassador and often did TV interviews, so her face was recognizable.

But something about the idea of meeting the woman face-to-face caused a rush of apprehension to sweep through Teagan. She quickly muttered hello as she sat across from the woman.

Monroe, as he'd introduced himself, stood beside Charlie. The man was big and broad like a linebacker. His jaw was hard and his eyes emotionless.

A bodyguard?

That was Teagan's best guess.

As soon as Charlie cast her a smile, Teagan's shoulders loosened.

"I know you had quite the ordeal to get here, but I'm glad you made it." Charlie handed her a water bottle before leaning back in her chair again, looking calm, cool, and in control. "And here's a muffin for you. Prickly pear flavored. It's one of our Chef Dean's favorite recipes. I know it sounds strange, but it's surprisingly good."

"Thank you for all you've done. I don't know how I can ever repay you." What Charlie was doing here at the ranch truly was amazing and life-changing on so many levels.

Teagan had given up on ever escaping from the Farinos.

Until she'd talked to Charlie.

She twisted the top from her water and took a long sip.

"There's no need to repay us," Charlie said. "We're just happy to help. Unfortunately, we do have some business to take care of. But if you're not feeling up to it, we can wait."

"We might as well get it over with," Teagan said.

Charlie remained silent another moment before slowly, purposefully nodding. "Of course. You're my kind of gal. I just like to rip off the Band-Aid, you know what I mean?"

"I do."

"Anyway, this is the way it works when people come here to Vanishing Ranch." Charlie held out her hand, tapping her fingers as she ticked things off. "We'll teach you everything you need to know to start a new life. We'll give you a new identity. A new place to live. Set you up with a new career. We'll practice the details with you so they all make sense before you leave. You'll sound natural when you talk to other people. We'll also teach you some self-defense skills just in case you need them."

"That sounds great." Even though Teagan said the words, she dreaded living them out. She didn't want to start over again, but she had no other choice.

If it was just her, maybe she wouldn't go through this agony.

But for the sake of her child, she would do whatever it took.

"I understand this won't be the first time you've done something like this." Charlie unapologetically studied Teagan's face.

Teagan glanced at Hudson. Of course, Hudson had told Charlie more details. He had to. Reporting updates to his boss was part of his job.

"I understand this whole situation is probably causing some type of PTSD with you." Charlie continued to observe Teagan, as if evaluating her mental state.

Teagan released a slow breath. "Maybe a little. I'm a bit overwhelmed."

"As anyone in your shoes would be."

Teagan shifted as reality continued to hit her. So much felt uncertain right now. She needed some time to find her center of balance.

"If you don't mind me asking, how long can I stay here and try to get myself together?"

Charlie's gaze locked with hers. "As long as you need."

After Teagan finished meeting with Charlie, Charlie instructed Hudson to give her a tour of the place.

He started in the mess hall, showing her the offices, a workout room, and introducing her to Chef Dean, Kota the housekeeper, and several ranch hands.

She was also introduced to the rest of the team.

Former FBI agent Jesse Marx had helped rescue her on the helicopter. The man was tall and thin with a messy hairstyle and cowboy-like bravado—even though Teagan sensed he wasn't really a cowboy.

Sienna, a petite blonde who used to be CIA, stood beside Jesse. The two of them continued to exchange glances with each other that made it clear they were head over heels about each other. Or, as Hudson had said, kind of married. Teagan had no idea what that meant.

Mateo Garcia looked tough with his tattoos, but his eyes said otherwise. He was a former *federales*—or what was officially known as the Mexican Policía Federal Ministerial.

They certainly had a top-notch team here. No one could argue that.

He then went outside and showed her the bunkhouse, the swimming pool, shooting range, and the cabanas near hers.

He saved his favorite place, the stable, for last.

Back when they'd been dating, he'd taught Teagan how to ride a horse. They'd gone on trail rides together, and she'd been a natural—the most beautiful cowgirl he'd ever seen.

"Wow." Teagan slowly wandered from stall to stall, admiring each horse. "Look at all these beauties."

Hudson lingered behind her. "We rescue horses as part of our cover. Plus, that's what funds the organization. Charlie has a great circle of donors who support her efforts."

She paused by Winnie, an appaloosa that had just come in last week. "What do you mean by rescue?"

"Sometimes horses are in bad situations with owners who just don't care anymore or who don't have the funds to support the animal's needs. Sometimes, the horses are willingly given up to us. Other times, we have to do rescue operations without the owner's consent."

"Really? I've never thought about covert horse rescues before. Is that even legal?"

"We go through all the proper legal means first. But if that doesn't work then we'll take matters into our own hands. Sometimes owners are so heartless that they don't care what's best for their horses."

She paused in front of one of the stalls.

Even after all this time had passed, she was still a knockout. The best part? She'd never even known it.

Back when he'd met her, she'd looked casual. She'd been down-to-earth. A curiosity about life had sparkled in her eyes.

"It sounds like good work you guys are doing—on more than one level."

Teagan's voice pulled him away from his thoughts. "We hope so."

"How did Charlie recruit you to come here?"

He shrugged. "When I was working for that government contractor I told you about, we had this gala that everyone was required to attend. Charlie was there. She'd done her research. She knew who I was and struck up a conversation with me. Asked me to come out and check out the ranch. Said she was hiring and knew I loved horses."

"She really does do her homework, huh?"

"Most definitely. I came out for an interview, and that's when she told me what she really does here. I accepted the job on the spot."

"Why does she want to do this?" Teagan crossed her arms and leaned against a wooden post.

"It's more than a job to Charlie. It's personal. I don't know details, but I know her mom was in a bad situation after her dad died. When Charlie was old enough and had the means, she decided that she wanted to help people in similar situations."

"It sounds noble." As she said the words, the horse beside her let out a loud neigh.

Teagan chuckled as she turned to the chestnut-colored animal.

"Does that mean you agree with me?" she murmured. "Who are you?"

"This is Bessy. She came to us about four months ago. Her owner wasn't feeding her. Her hooves were overgrown. Her skin was infected. She was in bad shape. Charlie ended up purchasing her from the owner. Sometimes, money is all it takes."

"Well, it's nice to meet you, Bessy. Charlie must have thought you were special," Teagan muttered as she leaned closer to the horse.

"She does . . . especially since Bessy is pregnant."

TEAGAN RUBBED the side of Bessy's face, feeling an instant kinship with the mare. An instinctive part of herself wanted to protect the horse—maybe in a way that Teagan couldn't protect herself.

Should she tell the people here at Vanishing Ranch about her pregnancy?

Part of her thought the answer should be an easy yes. But another part wanted to keep the secret to herself. The revelation was something no one could take from her or try to manipulate. It felt like her own little secret that she could rejoice in.

Then again, maybe the people around her needed to know. Her condition made it even more urgent that she stay safe. Above all, she had to think about her unborn child.

God was giving her a blessing. She'd fight with everything inside her to keep the child safe and protected.

Would her baby be a boy or a girl? Either way, Teagan loved this child with all her heart.

"Teagan?"

She swung her gaze toward Hudson and realized he must have said something to her.

She pushed a hair behind her ear, trying to compose herself. "Yes?"

He stared at her, confusion in his gaze. "Are you okay?"

She nodded, probably too quickly. "Yes, I'm fine. Sorry. Just tired. I was thinking about Miss Bessy here and everything she's been through. I actually volunteered at an animal shelter back in Dallas."

"Really? That doesn't fit everything else you've said about your time with the Farinos."

"I know. But Ricky convinced them they should let me. I started once a week about six months ago. Frank said it would look good for the family if I was out there doing charity work."

"So, he let you go by yourself?"

She shook her head. "No. Two guards always accompanied me and waited outside."

"Your coworkers at the shelter didn't ask any questions about that?"

Teagan let out a breath. "They knew who I was. Knew what family I'd come from. Angela, the director, seemed hesitant at first. I couldn't blame her. But eventually, she agreed. She slowly became one of my only friends."

"Angela did? That's good. I'm glad you had someone."

"I mean, we weren't friends in the sense that we went out or talked on the phone. But the two of us chatted when I came in to volunteer. I always thought that if I needed someone to reach out to, Angela could be that person. But I never wanted to put her in that position."

"That sounds tough."

Teagan nodded, swallowing back her emotions. "Anyway, you know I've always loved animals. I loved helping the dogs and cats at the shelter. I had a favorite —a Corgi named Daisy. I always asked if I could bring her home, but Ricky said no. In some strange way, I think he felt threatened by the dog."

"Really?" Hudson raised his eyebrows.

Teagan shrugged. "He had . . . issues. Anyway . . . I think what Charlie is doing here is great. Especially for horses like you, Bessy." She leaned closer to the horse as if whispering a secret.

Hudson looked back at the horse. "She's due any day now. Maybe you'll be here when she delivers. Have you ever seen a horse give birth?"

"No, I'm not like you. I didn't grow up on a ranch." No, she'd grown up as a military brat, right up until the time her father had been killed during an accident overseas.

Then it was just her and her mom. After moving a couple of times, they'd finally settled in the Los Angeles suburbs. Her mom had taken a job doing marketing for a small production company.

That's where Teagan had met Ricky. He'd been in town on a business trip from Chicago, his family's hub of operations. She hadn't known at the time what kind of illicit deal it was—it had apparently involved drugs. She hadn't even recognized the Farino last name.

No, all she'd seen was Ricky. She'd been drawn by his charisma and bright smile and good looks.

He'd been tall with olive skin and thick, dark hair. When he walked into a room, people noticed him, fawned over him.

He could snap his fingers and people did his bidding.

She'd never seen anything like it.

But slowly, that image had crumbled. She'd realized he was emotionally volatile. She'd realized his family's affairs were less than ethical.

She'd known she had to get out.

She couldn't envision a future with him.

He'd begged Teagan to change her mind. Said he couldn't go on without her.

But she hadn't budged.

"Watching one of these mares give birth is a beautiful sight." Hudson's voice pulled her from her thoughts.

Something about the idea intrigued her.

"That sounds amazing." She rubbed Bessy's face again. "Maybe you can find me when she goes into labor . . ."

"I'll do that." Hudson offered a quick grin as he stepped back. "Anyway, lunch will be served soon. Are you hungry?"

As if Teagan's stomach understood his question, a growl sounded. "As a matter of fact, I'm starving."

"I thought you might be." He nodded toward the doors. "Let's go get you something to eat."

Teagan almost wanted to add that she was eating for two. But she didn't let those words leave her mouth.

Not yet.

Even though part of her wanted to fall back into Hudson's arms and pick up where they'd left off, she knew that wasn't wise. Soon, she'd have a new identity and start over in a new place . . . without Hudson.

She needed to keep her distance.

If she was smart, she wouldn't forget that during her time here at the ranch.

———

Hudson saw the look on Teagan's face while they were in the stable, but he had no idea what she was thinking. Her expression almost signaled regret.

But why?

Did she regret leaving her old life behind? Regret being here? Regret seeing him again?

A lot could have changed in the two years they'd been apart.

He had trouble thinking that was true. But he also realized Teagan was keeping other secrets. He could see them in her gaze. He knew her well enough to read her expressions.

He hoped whatever those secrets were that they didn't affect anyone here at the ranch.

"Teagan?" He turned toward her.

Teagan snapped her gaze away from Bessy and glanced back at him, almost appearing reluctant to leave. "Sorry. I got lost in my thoughts."

Her hand dropped to her side, but her gaze remained on the horse, almost as if she didn't want to leave her.

Hudson had grown up around horses. He'd even done the rodeo circuit for a while, all the way up until he'd joined the Navy and had eventually become a SEAL.

He'd been stationed in San Diego, and Teagan had been working there as a travel writer for a magazine. For one of her assignments, she had gone to a traveling rodeo in town.

Hudson had been there also.

That was where he and Teagan had met.

When she accidentally walked behind a bucking horse and had almost been kicked, Hudson had pulled her out of the way.

She'd mesmerized him from that moment on.

Teagan had asked what she could do to say thank you, and Hudson had said she could have dinner with him.

Teagan had agreed, and they'd been inseparable

after that. Six months later, they'd gotten engaged. They'd planned on getting married that spring.

They never got the chance.

Instead, she'd died on her way to an overseas meeting when her plane had gone down in Mexico.

Obviously, that wasn't what really happened.

Now Hudson had to question what exactly *did* happen.

Teagan's stomach rumbled, bringing him from his thoughts.

"Sounds like you're ready for some food." He started to touch the small of Teagan's back as they headed toward the mess hall.

She flinched at his touch, and Hudson quickly withdrew his hand.

Clearly, they couldn't pick up where they left off. Not that he wanted to. Touching her had just seemed so natural.

Even if Teagan hadn't chosen to fake her death, that didn't mean Hudson would be able to forget the pain he'd gone through. It didn't mean that he could look past the secrets she still kept.

Even if everything in him wanted to.

At one time, Hudson had dreams about the two of them starting a life together at a ranch like this. He'd figured he would put in ten or fifteen years as a SEAL, and then he'd leave to enjoy some of the wide-open spaces he'd come to love while growing up in Montana.

Teagan had seemed on board with that. Those were

the plans they'd made together. The dreams they'd talked about.

He'd completely fallen apart when she had died. Because of his grief, he'd even decided to leave the military early. He wasn't in a good headspace, and that wasn't fair to his teammates. He'd known it was time to move on.

His lips tugged down in a frown as they headed toward the mess hall.

Even if Teagan couldn't have escaped the Farinos, she could've found some way to contact him, couldn't she? To let him know she was still alive. Didn't she trust him enough to think that he could take care of himself?

Then he remembered that scar Teagan had shown him.

He swallowed hard as regret and anger mingled inside him.

How could they do this to her?

Now that his surprise was beginning to fade, his emotions were shifting into anger—anger toward the Farinos.

Hudson wasn't normally an angry guy.

Still, it would take time to deal with this plot twist in his life.

Teagan also had a lot to deal with, however.

Over the next couple of weeks—if not longer—she would have to learn to be someone else . . . something that she clearly already had experience with. But it still wouldn't be easy on her.

For now, he'd take Teagan to the mess hall for lunch,

and then he'd figure out how he was going to handle these next few weeks.

As they continued walking that way, his phone buzzed with a text message from Charlie.

He pulled it from his pocket and glanced at the screen.

What he saw there took his breath away.

It was his face . . . on a wanted poster.

For the abduction of Kat Farino.

CHAPTER
SIXTEEN

THREE DAYS HAD PASSED since Teagan arrived at Vanishing Ranch.

Every day, she'd had meetings where she learned about her new identity and rehearsed the details of her new life so they could eventually come naturally.

She'd gone through self-defense courses, taking care not to endanger her baby.

She'd looked after Bessy—which had undoubtably been her favorite parts of her days.

She'd also dyed her hair back to her natural color—brown. Sienna had trimmed it for her, so it fell to her shoulders in waves.

Teagan looked—and felt—more like herself.

Hudson had been cordial to her, but he remained distant.

Not that Teagan could blame him.

Still, there was so much she wanted to say to him. To explain.

But at this point, she wasn't sure how much good it would do. She'd been forced to marry Ricky. Forced to go along with their scheme.

What was done was done.

Now, she had to think about herself and her baby.

Soon, she would be Tina Johnson. She'd be living in Florida, one of her least favorite states—but only because she hated humidity in the summer and crowds in the winter.

Would she really be safe there, tucked away in a small coastal town on the Gulf? Or would the Farinos find her?

The question haunted her. It terrified her to think of them swooping in and stealing away her child.

She couldn't let her mind go there.

For now, she finished getting ready for the day and then strode outside toward the mess hall for breakfast.

Even though Teagan had only been here a short time, she was already getting used to the dusty ground beneath her feet. She'd already come to appreciate the way the sun rose over the mountains in the distance, casting a purple hue on them even as the sky lit up with orange and yellow. She'd already come to treasure the wide-open expanses around her.

Her desolate surroundings almost made her feel like she could breathe. Like she could relax.

But she knew that would be a bad idea. Would she ever be able to fully unwind again?

As soon as she walked into the mess hall, the scent of bacon surrounded her.

Her favorite.

Before she could grab food and find a seat, Charlie motioned toward her from her office.

Teagan's gaze shifted, and she spotted Hudson standing beside Charlie.

A knot formed in her throat.

Something was up. She was certain of it.

Dread built inside her as she strode toward the office.

Hudson pulled out a chair in front of the desk and waited until she was seated before he lowered himself beside her. Then they both turned toward Charlie.

"I don't believe in withholding information from our guests here." Charlie's voice sounded stiff and serious, which only cranked Teagan's nerves tighter. "That's why I wanted to let you know a couple of things. First, the Farinos have pointed a finger at Hudson, claiming he abducted you. His picture is now featured on wanted posters throughout Texas."

Teagan sucked in a breath. "What?"

She glanced at Hudson for confirmation that she'd heard correctly.

He nodded but remained quiet.

"I've been on the phone with some of my law enforcement contacts trying to smooth this over," Charlie continued. "I'll do everything I can to clear his name—of course."

Teagan nodded, wishing that comforted her. But it didn't. Not yet.

"As I'm sure you know, the family is furious that

you're gone. Unfortunately, they are also offering a hundred-thousand-dollar reward for your safe return."

That wasn't a surprise.

Of course, they'd made it seem like they were concerned in-laws.

They were anything but.

"Publicly, they're saying you've been abducted. But I feel certain they know you played a part in this."

"Of course."

"We have connections out in the field, and we've told them to keep their ears open for anything new with the Farinos," Charlie continued.

"What does this mean for me now?" Teagan rubbed her hands on her jeans, hating the sticky feel of her palms.

Charlie shrugged, amazingly calm despite her concern. "Nothing really. We were aware when we agreed to let you come here that the Farinos were aggressive and would do everything within their power to find you."

Alarm raced through her. "Do you think they have any idea that I'm here?"

"No." Charlie said the word firmly, leaving no room for doubt. "Not only are we in the middle of nowhere, but we have people on the lookout for anyone who might come this way."

Teagan released the breath she held. "That's good news, at least."

"We'd like to keep you here at the ranch a little

longer than we initially anticipated. Right now, it feels too dangerous to send you off anywhere else."

Charlie's words drove home the reality of the situation. In other words, they feared for her life right now.

"I don't want to overstay my welcome." Teagan wasn't sure why she'd said that. Being courteous should be the least of her concerns. But it seemed a safer notion to talk about than the likelihood of her death.

"You won't be overstaying." Hudson sounded certain, as if he had no doubts.

"I can't stay forever." Her voice came out soft as she said the words. "Eventually, I'm going to have to go out into the real world."

Suddenly, that thought struck terror in her. She didn't want to be out there. Alone. She hadn't realized how safe she'd begun to feel with Hudson nearby until now.

This wasn't a vacation or a blip in her future.

There would be no going back to a normal life, would there?

Why had she ever thought her escape was possible? Whether physically or emotionally, she was always going to be a prisoner of the Farinos.

———

Teagan's words served as a good reminder of the reality of this situation, Hudson realized.

She was right. She couldn't stay here at Vanishing Ranch forever.

Neither could he.

Nothing had come of that wanted poster yet. It had been released throughout Texas.

Clearly, the man he'd fought off in the parking lot had done a sketch of him. The Farinos had recognized him and had decided to retaliate.

Charlie had called one of her contacts with the FBI—someone who knew what was going on. He'd told her he'd try to take care of it.

But still . . . that left Hudson in a precarious situation.

Staying here on the ranch was the safest option until all this blew over.

Since Hudson had come here to begin working a year ago, he'd noticed their guests stayed for two months on average. That usually gave them enough time to regroup and learn their new identity.

Once they were taken to the new location to begin their new lives, a Vanishing Ranch agent would accompany them to their new home and stay nearby for two weeks as they adjusted.

After that, their guests were on their own.

They were given an emergency number to use in case of extreme danger.

So far, no one had used the number—not that Hudson knew about, at least.

On occasion, their agents checked up on their guests and their new lives. They never made themselves known. But Charlie believed in staying on top of situations. And she believed in community.

That meant she didn't like leaving these women out on their own. But they couldn't do anything to put them at risk either.

The thought of Teagan being alone with the Farinos after her . . . he couldn't imagine ever letting her go into that situation.

"Anyway . . ." Charlie shifted forward and took a long sip of water. "You've been working hard since you arrived. I wondered if you might be interested in taking a horseback ride today."

"A horseback ride?" Teagan's eyes lit at the possibility. "I'd love to. I mean . . . as long as it's easy. I haven't ridden in a long time."

Charlie grinned. "Great. Hudson can take you. Sound good?"

A battle raged inside Hudson. Part of him wanted to spend time with her. The other part of him realized it would be better to keep his distance.

However, he was a professional. He could separate his emotions from this job.

"Of course. I'll get the horses saddled up. It's cool enough this morning that we should be able to get a decent ride in."

Thirty minutes later, Hudson and Teagan set out across the desert. He rode Bongo, and he'd given Teagan a stallion named Tom Brady. She'd had a good laugh over the horse's name. Monroe, a former football player himself, had named the horse.

Honestly, Hudson loved nothing more than these rides. He could do this all day.

He loved the Joshua trees and desert scrub. Just on the other side of this mountain range, Saguaro cacti arose like desert warriors guarding the land.

The one thing he had come to love about Arizona was how much the landscape changed every thirty miles or so. At least, that's how it seemed to him.

"Some of my favorite memories are from our trail rides together," Teagan murmured as they bounced along the dusty landscape toward the mountains in the distance.

He smiled despite himself. "Those were nice, weren't they?"

"Everything felt perfect in my world during those moments." Her smile slipped. "Remember when we used to talk about driving down Route 66?"

He wasn't sure he wanted to reminisce. But the memory *was* a good one.

"When I got out of the Navy, that's what we were going to do," he finally said. "Before I found a new job and we settled down."

A smile whispered across her lips. "That sounded amazing."

"Yes, it did. We're not terribly far from that route right now—and, by not far, I mean a few hours."

Teagan opened her mouth as if she wanted to say more, but she didn't.

Instead, a few minutes later, she said, "You look like a natural out here."

Hudson shrugged. "You know me. Horses and ranches . . . is there anything better?"

"Not for you."

Hudson's thoughts continued to wander.

He had so many questions for Teagan, questions about what had transpired in the time since they'd been apart. What better time to ask than now?

"Have you been in Dallas for the past two years?" he started.

"Yes, I have. Dallas isn't for me, but it's a great city. But you know I'm not much of a city girl."

No, she hadn't been. She'd always talked about her desire to live somewhere with a lot of land and maybe even have a small farm with some chickens and goats.

The woman he'd seen in Dallas—the one with the designer clothes and salon-styled hair—wasn't the Teagan he remembered.

But the one beside him now—the one with the well-worn jeans, with her hair pulled into a ponytail, and almost no makeup . . . that was who he'd fallen in love with.

As the trail sloped, Hudson pointed to an area up ahead. "Nudge Tom Brady with your heels so he'll pick up speed as he goes across this riverbed."

Teagan did as he asked.

But as the stallion climbed the other side of the riverbed, Teagan suddenly lurched forward. Her hand went to her stomach.

Alarm raced through Hudson.

Something was wrong.

SEVENTEEN

AS TEAGAN FELT HERSELF CRAMPING, panic raced through her. Maybe coming on this horseback ride was a bad idea. But she'd figured it was early enough in her pregnancy that she should be fine.

What if she was wrong?

Almost as soon as the pain began, it faded.

She drew in a deep breath as she straightened and tried to compose herself.

But she knew it was too late.

Hudson had already seen her.

He quickly trotted up beside her and took her horse's reins as they paused. "What happened?"

"Nothing." She waved a hand in the air. "I just had a cramp."

He narrowed his gaze as he studied her. "Are you sure? You looked like you were in pain. We have a doctor we can call who'll come out here—"

"I think it's just the stress of everything. I'm fine."

But was she? Maybe she should be checked out.

She'd wait and see if the pain came again. If it did, she'd talk to Charlie.

Right now, there was no reason to assume the worst.

"Maybe we should get back," Hudson suggested.

Teagan wanted more than anything to explore and to continue enjoying the fresh air.

But Hudson was right. They should get back.

Just in case.

He handed her the reins, his gaze lingering on her a moment.

How long could she hide her pregnancy from him? Could she keep it quiet until she left here and started her new life? Maybe Hudson would never have to know.

Unless she started showing. So far, she only had a small bump. But she knew that would be changing in the coming months.

She didn't want to see the hurt in Hudson's eyes when she told the truth—because she was supposed to marry him, not Ricky. She'd been in the middle of a terrible situation, and she'd done what she could to survive.

And that had meant marrying Ricky. Maybe a small part of her had loved him.

Not like she loved Hudson. Not anywhere close.

But would Hudson ever understand that?

If she were in his shoes, she couldn't say she would.

The thoughts continued to pound inside her as they headed back to the ranch.

As they did, she prayed for her baby's health and safety.

She'd never forgive herself if she did something to put her child in danger.

Teagan never thought she'd say it, but she missed her phone. She knew why she couldn't have it. The reasoning made perfect sense.

But she wanted to know what was going on outside the ranch.

What exactly were her in-laws doing in an effort to find her?

They'd made people believe that Hudson had abducted her, for starters.

Anger burned through her at that thought.

How could they sink so low?

But she knew how. That was just their nature.

They'd ruined Teagan's life. Now they wanted to ruin Hudson's as well.

She lay in her bed, trying to get some rest. She hadn't felt any more cramps since she'd returned from the horseback ride. She hadn't had any bleeding.

So she thought she was okay.

If she had access to her phone or computer, she would have probably Googled it. But right now, all she had to go on were her instincts.

She placed her hand over her belly and lifted another prayer. She went through the act several times a day. Because she knew that without God, she had no hope of getting through this situation safely. Her faith had been all she'd had over these past two years.

She ran through the details of her new life in her mind. Her new name. The new place she would live. The new job she'd have.

Soon, she'd be a single mom.

Teagan knew she wouldn't ever be able to leave her child in daycare. Not because she thought it was wrong. But because she wouldn't trust anybody else to take care of her child, not with the Farinos still out there.

That meant she'd need to find work she could do at home. Writing would be too obvious.

The Farinos would find her that way.

But there were other things she could do.

Most likely, she'd need to isolate at her new home. To become a hermit.

That's what she would do if she had to in order to stay safe.

But Teagan had never really liked being alone. She had always enjoyed being around people.

Even though the Farinos had been a nightmare, she knew that as long as she treated Ricky nicely that he would keep her safe.

But now he was gone. And so was her safety net.

Someone knocked on her door, and she sat up.

"Come in," she called.

The door opened, and Hudson stood there. "I just came by to make sure you're okay."

When Teagan heard the concern in his voice, she wanted to melt.

She quickly moved her hand from over her stomach. If she kept making slipups like that, Hudson would put the pieces together and realize she was pregnant.

"I'm okay. I think it's just the stress of everything."

He nodded. "I'm glad it's nothing more. I thought I'd let you know that Bessy is about to give birth."

She sat up straighter. "What?"

"Do you want to see?"

"Can I?"

He let out a little laugh as if surprised by her excitement. "Of course, you can. Come on."

HUDSON STEPPED BACK to watch Bessy and her baby.

Labor had lasted three hours, and Hudson had been the one to help deliver the foal.

He hadn't had to do much. Nature did most of the work.

But he'd been on hand to help if needed. He'd suited up in gloves and an apron.

Basically, he was filthy. But he didn't care.

He only cared about the fact that mama and baby were fine.

He glanced at Teagan as the foal stood on wobbly legs.

She stared at the scene, shaking her head and with a look of awe in her gaze. Using her shirt sleeve, she wiped the moisture from her eyes.

"You have to excuse me." She fanned her face as

more tears filled her gaze. "That was just so beautiful. Is her baby okay?"

"He looks like a fine healthy boy." Hudson stared at the quarter horse with its creamy brown skin and a strip of white across his nose. "He's going to be strong, just like his mama."

Tears continued to spring to Teagan's eyes. "I don't know why I'm crying. I've just never seen anything like that before."

"It is quite the experience."

"How long was Bessy pregnant?"

"Eleven months and a few days. Her baby weighs about a hundred pounds."

"Wow. She's one tough mother."

Hudson grinned. "She is."

"And Bessy's doing okay?" She started to reach for the new mama but stopped herself as if unsure that was okay in this situation.

"You can touch her face. It's fine."

Teagan gently ran her hand down Bessy's cheek. "You're such a strong girl. You did amazing."

He held back a smile. Teagan definitely seemed to feel a bond with the horse.

He'd always known that horses could be healing.

That was one of the reasons he liked to work with them so much.

They'd certainly kept him out of trouble when he was a kid.

Where he'd grown up in Montana, there wasn't much to do. A lot of his friends had turned to drinking, drugs, and partying. Taking care of his horses had given Hudson purpose and kept him busy.

"Thank you for letting me witness this." Teagan glanced up at him, gratitude in her gaze. "I'll never forget it."

"Of course. I knew you'd want to see it."

She nodded, her cheeks unusually flushed.

"Would you like to name him?" he asked.

Teagan's eyebrows shot up. "Me? Name him?"

He chuckled again. "Yes, you."

She glanced back at the foal. "I'd love that. How about Jitterbug?"

His eyebrows shot up this time. "Jitterbug?"

She shrugged. "It fits him with the way he's jumping all over the place right now."

"I like it. Jitterbug it is."

She smiled, looking the happiest Hudson had seen her since she'd arrived here.

The realization brought him a burst of joy.

He pushed the emotion down and turned his thoughts back to his mission. "Now, I need to leave Mateo in charge so I can get cleaned up."

"Of course. Don't mind me. Can I stay a little bit longer?" She glanced at him, her eyes hopeful.

Hudson grinned again. "Of course. I think Bessy— and Jitterbug—would like that."

The next morning, Teagan visited with Bessy and Jitterbug again. She was slightly obsessed with the horses.

Afterward, she wandered into the mess hall for breakfast.

Despite her better instincts, she found herself searching the crowd for Hudson.

She spotted him lingering in the doorway to Charlie's office, so she headed that way.

She paused as she got closer. A TV blared in the corner of the room, a newscaster reciting today's headlines.

A familiar name caught her ear, and her blood went cold.

"Police are searching for twenty-eight-year-old Angela Stevens, who disappeared two nights ago. Friends say she left work at the animal shelter she runs and hasn't been seen or heard from since. If you have any information or if you have seen Angela Stevens, please call . . ."

Teagan must have gasped because everyone in the office turned to look at her.

"That's my friend," she murmured.

Hudson glanced back at the TV. "The woman who was just on the news?"

Teagan nodded, remembering her friend's honey-blonde hair, her tanned cheeks, her friendly smile. "Angela was the director at the animal shelter where I volunteered. She was my only friend outside the family, but I didn't think the Farinos knew that. I tried to keep my secret but . . ." Her voice cracked, and she placed a hand over her mouth as worst-case scenarios pummeled her.

"They always had someone watching," Hudson finished.

"They took Angela to send me a message." Her voice sounded strained as she said the words.

"That sounds like the Farinos," Charlie muttered. "This is a Dallas news station. I was watching to see if anything was being reported about your disappearance."

Teagan's heart pounded harder as she thought it through.

She *had* to help her friend.

But she also had to protect her baby.

How could she possibly do both?

"We'll see what we can find out." Charlie picked up a pen and clicked it in her hands. "In the meantime, sit tight. I've hired some of the best in the business here. We *will* find some answers for you."

Teagan turned away, hoping that neither Charlie nor Hudson could see the doubt in her gaze.

Because she knew better than anyone just how cruel the Farinos could be.

What if they'd already hurt her friend?

How would Teagan live with herself if that were the case?

CHAPTER
NINETEEN

HUDSON WATCHED as Teagan walked away. He wanted to follow, but he knew it was best to give her some space. Best for both of them.

Instead, he turned back to Charlie. "Did you know about this?"

She shook her head as she glanced at the TV screen again. "I didn't realize Teagan and this Angela woman were friends. There were no indications this would happen."

"Clearly, the local police are looking into this." Monroe shifted, crossing then uncrossing his arms. "But I can send someone out. We can do our own investigating."

"Did you see the look in Teagan's eyes?" Hudson asked. "She would do anything to protect the people she loves. That's why she married Ricky in the first place. Because the Farinos threatened me."

"If you're worried about her running, there's no

easy way for her to get away from this place," Charlie said.

"But she might die trying." His words hung in the air.

A frown flickered across Charlie's face. "Keep an eye on her. I'll get someone on this right away so maybe we can give her some peace of mind. I'll need to talk to her later after we do some of our own research."

A bad feeling churned in Hudson's stomach. He understood where Charlie was coming from.

But Charlie didn't know Teagan like he did.

The Farinos had known exactly what card to play. They'd known that threatening someone Teagan cared about was the only way to get her to come out of hiding.

But why did they want to get her back so badly? Did they consider her their property?

Hudson wasn't sure how much sense that made. Ricky had been the one they'd cared about. Teagan was just someone who'd made their son happy.

Instantly, Hudson heard a mental clock ticking and pressure began building between his shoulder blades.

If there was any hope of saving Teagan, they would need to resolve this ASAP.

Teagan couldn't sit still. She'd attempted to eat some oatmeal, but the food felt like cement in her stomach.

Instead, she'd escaped outside to clear her head.

She'd paced along the fence near the horse pasture for a while before stopping and leaning against the wooden enclosure.

It was already hot out, but not as hot as it would get later in the day. Besides, she didn't care about the heat.

All she cared about right now was Angela.

Angela had felt like a friend from the moment Teagan met her. Angela had started and run the animal rescue. She just wanted to take care of animals that others had abandoned. She had a knack for it.

The two had never gone out for dinner or coffee like normal friends might. That would have been too risky. Instead, Teagan had come into work early on occasion so they could talk and catch up.

Angela was single, and that shelter was her whole life. It wasn't unusual to find her friend sitting on the floor in one of the kennels, holding an animal who'd just come in and trying to comfort it.

Teagan's heart lurched into her throat at the memories.

Why hadn't Teagan even considered that the Farinos might do this? Of *course*, they would. The Farinos would try every trick in the book to bring Teagan pain, to bring her back home.

Tears pressed at her eyes, but she pulled them back.

She couldn't let herself go there.

Yet all of her emotions were so much more vivid since her pregnancy. She had trouble holding them at bay anymore.

"Hey," a deep voice said behind her.

She knew without turning who it was.

Hudson.

He joined her by the fence, resting his arms on the wooden post and staring at the horses as they nibbled hay that had been placed in the pasture. "Our team is working on your friend's disappearance right now. We'll probably have more questions for you later."

"Whatever I can do. I want to help."

"I know you do. And I know this has been hard on you."

"Being here has made it easier." She flashed a soft smile, not wanting to sound ungrateful.

A few moments of silence passed before Hudson cleared his throat. "I didn't realize when we first met that when you said you'd broken up with someone that he was a member of the Farino family. You never mentioned that."

She shrugged, not surprised that he wanted more details. They still had so much to talk about. "I was trying to escape the memories. It's why I moved to San Diego. To get away from it all. But it didn't work. Trouble followed me."

"Was it horrible being married to Ricky?"

Hudson's question took her by surprise. Teagan took a moment to think about it before answering.

"Ricky really thought he loved me," she finally said. "He wouldn't let anyone hurt me. And he didn't hurt me either. In fact, he kept me safe from his family. But I felt trapped. I was in a situation with no way out."

"Until he died."

A lump formed in her throat.

"Yes, until he died." Her voice came out just above a whisper. "I was at a luncheon with some ladies in the family. When I returned home—bodyguard in tow—I found Ricky in the kitchen with a bullet in his head. Blood was everywhere."

Hudson squeezed her arm. "You don't have to finish. I'm sorry to bring it up . . ."

"No, it's okay. It was a terrible sight to see. But it's over and done with now."

"Do the Farinos know who's responsible?"

"Thankfully, I was at a luncheon with the other ladies in the family, so they couldn't blame me. Otherwise, I'm sure I would have been a suspect. Instead, they thought it was one of the McConnells—a rival family. Before twenty-four hours were up, two more people were dead. The Farinos sent a message to the McConnells, setting off a war of sorts."

Hudson's jaw visibly tightened. "I can imagine."

"I never knew what evil was until I met this family. After that, I knew I had to get away. I couldn't keep living like that."

When an FBI agent had questioned Teagan about what happened, he'd slipped her a card with a phone number. He'd whispered, "If you need help, call them."

She hadn't done so right away. Instead, she'd pondered if she should.

On more than one occasion, she'd started to call and then stopped herself.

But finally, one day while she was volunteering at

the animal shelter, she'd used Angela's phone and had called. She knew she couldn't use her own. That the Farinos would monitor her calls. So, she'd told Angela her own phone had died, and Angela hadn't seemed to question her statement.

Teagan had truly thought the Farinos hadn't known Angela was her friend.

The next morning, a burner phone appeared in her mailbox. Only one number was programmed into it, and she dialed it. That's when she'd talked to Charlie and this whole process had begun.

She glanced at Hudson, questions racing through her head. "How many contacts do you guys have out there helping you find women who need help?"

She'd wondered how this whole process worked.

Hudson shrugged. "Maybe thirty. Charlie is very selective as to who she lets know about what we're doing. If everyone knew, then Vanishing Ranch wouldn't be a secret, and therefore it wouldn't be effective. So, Charlie only lets people she trusts know, and people who are in contact with women who might need assistance. The FBI. Police officers. A couple of doctors. Some women's shelters."

"How does she even have those connections?"

"She worked as an ambassador for a while. Plus, she's a mover and a shaker. She's great at networking and getting people to rally behind her."

"It's wonderful what she's doing. I met Melanie during dinner one day this week. She told me her story, and I know that you guys are saving her life by allowing her to come here." Melanie's husband was a cop, and she'd come close to losing her life more than once.

She would probably be dead if she hadn't been brought here.

Just then, Monroe called to them. Teagan glanced back and saw him standing at the door to the mess hall. He motioned for them to come inside.

Teagan's breath caught.

Did they have an update on Angela?

She was about to find out.

MONROE LED Teagan and Hudson into a conference room and directed them to sit.

Papers had been strewn across the table as well as a map with several marked locations, and a laptop rested in front of Charlie.

Teagan felt anxiety rippling inside her as she anticipated what was about to transpire.

Jesse and Mateo were also there.

Charlie wasted no time getting started. "We know a little bit more now than we did when we talked to you last. Our contacts in Dallas indicated that Angela was last seen leaving the shelter at 9:23 p.m. two nights ago. They've tried to trace her location with the GPS on her car. However, it appears Ms. Stevens drove an older model with no built-in GPS."

Teagan nodded. "That's right. Running the animal shelter doesn't pay her very well, but she loves it."

"The last place her phone pinged was about an hour

outside of Dallas." Monroe pointed to the map and to a location. "Is anything about that area familiar to you?"

Teagan stared at it a few minutes. "Not necessarily. That's not the same direction as the Farino compound if that's what you're asking."

"No, we knew it wasn't." Charlie frowned. "But we figure the family has more than one location where they like to meet. Do you know where any of those other properties might be?"

Teagan let out a breath, and her eyes wandered back and forth as if in thought. "I did go to a couple of other places. But honestly, I feel like Frank is too smart to take Angela to any of those locations. Then again, the police probably have no clue that the Farinos could be involved in her disappearance. On paper, she probably has no connections to them."

Except for me.

Teagan kept those thoughts quiet.

"They don't yet," Charlie said. "I won't drop their names to our contact—not without you being okay with it."

"I appreciate that." Teagan sucked in another long breath before wiping her sweaty palms against her jeans. "What else do you need to know in the meantime?"

"Is it like Angela to take off?" Charlie asked.

Teagan shook her head. "No, it's not. She loves those animals, and she wouldn't do anything to put them in danger. Did she even have someone lined up to come take her place the next morning?"

"My understanding is that she did not," Charlie said. "However, another volunteer showed up around 10 a.m., and all the animals are fine. They just had a few messes to clean up in the meantime."

"That's good to know because it would break Angela's heart if anything happened to them."

"You said the Farinos didn't know anything about Angela?" Hudson shifted in his seat as he studied Teagan.

She nodded. "I was certain not to talk about her. But, like I said, the Farinos have eyes and ears everywhere."

"So, you didn't do anything with Angela outside of work?" Hudson stared at her from across the table.

"I didn't want to put her in that position." Teagan drew in a slow breath. "But we did just get a new volunteer at the shelter only two weeks ago. Art Lansdown was his name. He seemed kind of out of place and quiet, but I figured he was shy and awkward. Now that all of this has happened, I wonder if the Farinos planted him there to keep an eye on me."

Hudson's stomach tightened. That sounded exactly like something that they would do.

Charlie leaned forward, palms pressed into the table. "I'd like to see if we can narrow down some places where they may have taken her. Is there anywhere else that you might be able to think of?"

"I'm not sure," Teagan said. "But I'd be more than happy to tell you everything I know. Whatever you need to find her."

Her words hung in the air.

Hudson had no doubt she meant them.

Teagan would risk everything to help her friend . . . and that was exactly what he feared.

Teagan leaned back in her chair at the conference table, her thoughts racing.

She'd rattled off the addresses of four of the houses she knew of where the Farinos spent time. One was in Dallas, another in Chicago, a third in LA, and another in New York City.

But, as she had told the team earlier, she honestly believed the family was too smart to take Angela to any of those places. The Farinos hadn't grown their empire by making stupid mistakes. They knew how to cover their tracks.

That also meant they wouldn't take Angela anywhere where they didn't have some type of control. They wouldn't take her to a rental house or a motel— provided they were keeping her alive.

Teagan felt certain that they were.

They needed Angela alive in order to try to get Teagan to emerge.

"Anything?" Hudson's voice pulled her away from her thoughts.

"Not yet." She pressed her eyes shut, searching her memories for anything that might be a good lead.

Finally, she stopped at one idea.

She opened her eyes, and her gaze met Charlie's.

"One time, Ricky took me to a cabin in the middle of the woods in eastern Texas. Maybe I'm overthinking this, but I remember him saying something about how you never know when you might need a place off the grid. I asked him a few questions, and he said the property was purchased through a shell corporation and that his family went there sometimes when they needed to close a deal."

"Close a deal?" Charlie repeated.

Teagan shrugged. "I figured it was better if I didn't know. But the location is close to Dallas, and it's secluded. I think it's a really good possibility they took her there."

Charlie straightened. "Do you know the address?"

"No. I don't even think Ricky mentioned the address. I only went once."

"Can you tell us how to get there?" Hudson leaned closer as he waited for her answer.

Teagan shook her head. "No. I don't think I could. But . . . I could probably take you there."

TWENTY-ONE

HUDSON FELT a surge of protectiveness rush through him as he and Teagan climbed aboard Ghost's private jet. To say this mode of transportation was nice would be an understatement.

No expense had been spared—especially since Ghost usually used this for his private flights with celebrities and political leaders. The seats were leather, and all the finishings felt plush and expensive.

As Hudson lowered himself into the seat across from Teagan, he cast her a look. "For the record, I still think this is a terrible idea."

"It's the only option we have right now." Teagan buckled her seatbelt before turning toward him. "I don't know what else to do."

He swallowed hard before admitting the truth. "I don't want you to get hurt."

"I'll just show you the way to the area, and then I'll back off. I promise."

She sounded sincere. Sounded like that's really what she would do.

But Hudson had seen situations turn sideways before. He knew the danger they were getting themselves into.

And he didn't like it.

Several minutes later, they taxied down the runway, and Ghost took flight. Mateo had also come, but his other teammates were busy with another extraction.

Teagan glanced around the plane, her gaze curious. "I know you said Charlie raises money to run the ranch. But this plane . . . it's fancy."

Hudson nodded, thankful for the subject change. "It belongs to Ghost."

A wrinkle formed between her eyebrows. "Impressive."

Hudson's gaze met hers as he sat across from her in a padded beige chair. "He was a Navy fighter pilot. He then went on to be a commercial pilot, but he hated it. He began doing private charters later, and he bought this. Whenever he can help, he will."

"So, he doesn't do this full time?"

"No, his full-time job is flying celebrities from place to place. It pays the bills. But he's a good guy. He wants more out of his life than that."

"This makes more sense now."

Teagan glanced out the window a moment and then asked, "What are you going to do if you find Angela?"

"We'll need to get a feel for the situation first. If there are just one or two people guarding her, we should be able to take them out. If there are several people, then we may need to get the police involved. It's too early to say."

She nodded before looking back out the window.

Hudson had imagined her last flight many times before.

Imagined her on a small private jet taking off for a business trip to Brazil.

Had imagined her fear as the plane had signaled distress. As she realized they were in trouble. As the plane began to nosedive into the mountains of Mexico.

The images had replayed in Hudson's mind time and time again as he imagined her final moments. They'd haunted him since the day he'd gotten the news.

But that scenario hadn't been what happened at all.

He studied Teagan's face, wondering how much she knew about the crash.

"Who was the woman on the plane?" His question cut into the silence.

Teagan glanced at him, surprise in her gaze. "What?"

"The authorities found the plane crash. Found four bodies inside. Including a woman they believed to be you. Who was she?"

Teagan lowered her gaze before shaking her head. "I have no idea. I've often wondered that myself. My best guess is that the plane was loaded with people who'd somehow betrayed the Farinos. From what I overheard, the pilot ejected from the plane and let it crash. What they did was horrible."

Hudson had the urge to reach over and squeeze Teagan's hand, but he didn't. Not now. He shouldn't ever.

"We had a funeral for you." His voice cracked as he said the words.

She licked her lips as she stole a glance at him. Her hair fell into her gaze as she looked down, clearly grieved by what had happened. "I know. I'm so sorry you had to go through that."

He wanted to push that lock of hair out of her face, but he stopped himself. "I just wish you had contacted me."

"They were watching my every move. I had to be very careful. Wait for the right opportunity. They would have killed you if they found out I was trying to find you."

"Wait. So, you did try?"

She slowly nodded. "When I started volunteering at the animal shelter. But by then you had . . . vanished. I didn't know how to get in touch with you."

Hudson opened his mouth, but no reply came out.

That must have been when he'd started working at the ranch.

His gut clenched. If only he had known . . .

He could only imagine how difficult that would've been for Teagan.

She had searched for him. And he hadn't been there.

He couldn't help but wonder how things would be different right now if they'd simply been able to connect and find a safe place to talk two years ago.

Teagan saw the sorrow in Hudson's gaze, and her chest squeezed.

All the memories from the past came rushing back to her.

She'd had a business trip she had to go on.

Hudson would be out late the night before, so they'd already said goodbye to each other, knowing that she would need to be at the airport by 5:30 a.m. Normally he would drive her, but her work was going to send a car for her. It was better if he could get some rest in.

Teagan had halfway expected him to show up at her apartment anyway to surprise her and give her a ride to the airport himself.

Maybe he had. Maybe he'd come to pick her up and she wasn't there.

She didn't know.

By then it was too late.

The Farinos already had her.

When she'd returned home that evening to pack, Ron Farino—Frank's younger brother—had been waiting inside her apartment.

She'd had no warning.

Ricky hadn't called asking to get back together with her. She'd assumed he was in her past.

Apparently, the Farinos had other ideas.

Ron had shown her a live video feed of a gun

aiming at Hudson's back as he sat at a baseball game with his Navy SEAL buddies.

Ron insisted if she didn't come with him, that they were going to pull the trigger.

So, she had agreed.

Ron had watched as Teagan packed her bags just as she would for a normal business trip. She'd been able to take her laptop and her phone, her purse, several changes of clothing.

When they hadn't been looking, Teagan had slipped a picture of her and Hudson into one of the compartments in her suitcase. To her surprise, the Farinos had never discovered it. She'd simply found different hiding locations for it once Farino's men had gotten rid of that original suitcase and bought her designer luggage instead.

Ron had stayed with her all night, and then they'd left in what appeared to be a company car the next morning.

To anyone watching, everything would have appeared normal. The Farinos had covered their tracks.

Ron had driven her from San Diego and had kept driving. And kept driving.

Until they reached Dallas—where the family had just set up a base of operations. They hoped Ricky would oversee their new facilities.

Ricky had been waiting for her with his arms wide open as if her appearance was the most natural and normal thing in the whole world.

However, it was anything but.

Teagan had cried for weeks afterward. Could barely eat. Hadn't slept.

It was a living nightmare.

"It's the Grand Canyon."

She snapped from her thoughts and looked at Hudson. "What?"

He pointed out the window. "The Grand Canyon. That's where our road trip on Route 66 was going to end."

Despite herself, she smiled. "It's beautiful."

"Seeing it from up in the air is one of my favorite things. You can really take in the scope of it from up here. But when you're standing on the edge of it, you only can see what your surroundings will allow you to."

"It's amazing."

"It is."

He leaned close. Something about the action made her skin warm.

If only Teagan could go back in time and be held in Hudson's arms again.

But she couldn't.

Now she needed to stop thinking about all the ways it used to be.

She needed to get herself ready to find Angela.

CHAPTER
TWENTY-TWO

ONCE IN DALLAS, they picked up a car, and Teagan directed them away from the city and into the hill country.

Hudson's heart raced as they traveled.

He had to get himself focused. Distractions would only get them killed out here. But he couldn't stop thinking about the look on Teagan's face when she'd told him about what had happened.

She'd looked tormented.

"Do you think the Farinos know we're here?" Teagan's soft voice cut through the quiet.

"They shouldn't," Hudson told her. "They shouldn't have any way to trace us."

"Yet they always seem to," she muttered as she stared out the window, a forlorn expression on her face.

He wanted to argue, but he couldn't. However, every way he examined the situation, there was no way these guys should know Teagan was here.

Unless they had someone at the airport watching every flight that came and went.

Hudson's spine stiffened at the thought.

The Farinos very well could assume that Teagan would come back to look for Angela. Had they paid off someone who worked at various airports in the area? Did they have that much foresight?

Even if they had, these guys shouldn't be able to track Teagan down now. She'd changed her hair color as well as worn a baseball hat and sunglasses. The flight plans had been carefully written so no one would know where they landed.

So why did a bad feeling linger in his stomach?

Maybe it was because he knew these people had taken Angela for the sole purpose of getting Teagan back.

With Ricky dead, maybe they simply wanted to retaliate. Maybe they really did see her as their property.

"This is the exit we took." Teagan pointed to a sign ahead.

Hudson snapped from his thoughts as he glanced at the street sign.

Mateo turned at the exit just as Teagan directed.

"Do you remember how much farther this place is from here?" Hudson asked.

Teagan nibbled on her lip before saying, "Probably another hour, if I remember correctly. I just need to look for landmarks. I meant it when I said I couldn't tell you how to get here. For me, it's all a matter of visual memory."

Shoulders still tight, Hudson leaned back in the seat and waited for her next direction.

He'd done everything he could do to prepare for this. Now, all he could do was wait. And continue to pray their plan would succeed.

Memories battered Teagan.

This was one of the last places Ricky had taken her. Four months ago.

He'd wanted to plan a romantic getaway.

At that point in their relationship, Teagan had grown more comfortable around him. She wasn't necessarily happy, but she'd accepted her fate.

And Ricky had changed some in the time they'd been married.

Their stay at the cabin had actually been pleasant. The two of them had sat in front of the fireplace and drank hot chocolate and talked about what life would be like if Ricky didn't carry the Farino name.

It was the first time Teagan had ever heard Ricky talk about that. Until then, she'd assumed he was proud to be a part of his family.

But getting away from all of them—he'd even left the bodyguards at home—had seemed to make him relax a little more. To open up.

He'd admitted he'd had other dreams—of being a

lawyer, actually. That he didn't like the pressure from his family. That he didn't approve of their actions.

It had been refreshing to know he felt that way.

Did anyone in the family know that he'd talked about leaving?

Was that why he had been shot and killed?

Moisture welled in her gaze again. Even though Teagan hadn't truly loved Ricky, she couldn't get the image of his dead body out of her head.

He didn't deserve to die like that. In some ways, he was also a victim.

Who would have killed him? One of the Farinos' enemies? Or someone from within the family?

A chill swept through her at the thought.

She remembered when he'd proposed. It had happened only two months after her abduction, and he'd done it in front of his family.

She'd known she couldn't say no.

So she accepted Ricky's proposal.

But the next night when she'd tried to run . . .

That's when she'd been captured. When they'd put a knife to her chest.

For a brief moment, she'd been tempted to let them kill her rather than live in this kind of prison.

But she knew she couldn't do that. As long as she was alive, there was still hope.

Ron had roughed her up, told the family she'd been in an accident while riding her bike.

Everyone seemed to buy it.

Then he'd shown her pictures of Hudson. Hudson

with another woman. Ron had claimed that Hudson had moved on. That there was no reason for Teagan to leave now. That she had nothing and no one to run to.

She'd believed him for a while. But as soon as she started volunteering at the animal shelter, she'd looked Hudson up. She'd discovered the woman he was with was the wife of one of his SEAL teammates. They were only friends.

At that moment, she'd decided to contact Hudson. To beg for his help.

But he'd gone off-grid. He had no social media. His old number didn't work. He had no address.

Teagan hadn't been able to come up with another way to find him.

She had no way of knowing he'd started working at Vanishing Ranch. Nor had she ever heard of the place.

Three months later, she'd married Ricky in a small ceremony at his parents' estate in Chicago.

All because she had felt trapped with no way out.

"I think we're getting close," she said as she spotted a red house set back from the road with a stream running beside it.

Mateo sat up straighter as he drove.

"This is our next turn," she told the guys. "At this dirt road to the right."

"You'll need to let us know before we get to the house," Hudson said. "We can't just drive up there."

"I think there's one more turn up ahead until you reach the driveway. The driveway itself is probably a half mile long. So maybe before we get to the next turnoff, that would be a great place to park and hide your vehicle, just in case."

Hudson nodded. "Sounds good. We'll do that."

Anxiety churned inside her as Teagan imagined how things were going to play out next.

CHAPTER
TWENTY-THREE

HUDSON TURNED to Teagan after they'd hidden their car in the woods. "You need to stay here."

As he stared at her, he halfway expected to see rebellion in her gaze.

Instead, she nodded compliantly. "I will."

"Promise me." Hudson didn't look away until Teagan nodded again.

"I promise. The last thing I want to do is to slow you up. If my memory serves me correctly, the cabin is at the top of this hill. The property is secluded. I'm not even sure if you can see it overhead because of the trees."

"We've got this. There's a cell phone in the glovebox, but service is spotty out here. Still, if anything happens, you can try it."

"Got it."

"We'll be back as soon as we can." Hudson reached

into his bag, grabbed something, and then pressed it into her hand. "Use this if you need to."

Teagan glanced at the gun, and her eyes widened. "You want me to shoot somebody?"

"You remember how to use a handgun, right?" He'd taught her back when they'd been together. They'd gone to the gun range on more than one occasion.

"I . . . I think so."

"Don't be afraid to pull the trigger if someone threatens you."

After a moment of reluctance, Teagan nodded. "Okay."

Hudson had the urge to lean forward and press a quick kiss on her forehead. But he didn't. It wasn't his right, nor was it wise right now.

Instead, he turned toward Mateo. "Let's go."

They took off toward the cabin through the thick cover of trees.

If these guys were there, he would guess they had someone watching this property. Maybe cameras.

Either way, he and Mateo needed to be on guard.

They moved carefully, watching every step. Hudson's hand hovered near the gun at his hip. He had finely tuned instincts and skills and would draw if he had to.

Best-case scenario was that Angela was inside with only one or two men watching her. He and Mateo could take out those guards.

Then they could rescue Angela and bring her to Vanishing Ranch. There was no other choice. The woman would remain a target as long as the Farinos were out there.

Worst-case scenario, a whole army of men was waiting for Hudson and Mateo to show up so they could attack.

Hudson didn't know exactly what he and Mateo were going into right now. But he'd let the rest of his team know where they were so they should be able to pin his location in case something happened.

He hated to leave Teagan alone, but he couldn't bring her along either.

Their other team members were busy working on another extraction right now or he would have left someone with her.

She should be safe in the car. She had a gun if she needed it. Hudson prayed she wouldn't hesitate to use the weapon if someone threatened her.

They continued climbing up the rocky ground until they reached the top.

He paused as a cabin came into view.

This was where things got tricky.

***

Teagan knew that only fifteen minutes had passed.

But it felt like hours.

Every time the wind blew or a squirrel scampered by, her entire body tensed with dread and fear.

She slouched low in her seat in case anyone happened to see the vehicle. But Mateo had pulled far enough off the side of the road so that shouldn't be the case.

However, Teagan wouldn't let down her guard.

Instead, she stared at the gun in her hands.

Her stomach squeezed at the feel of the cold, heavy metal.

She hoped she didn't have to use this thing.

It was hard enough to pull the trigger with the gun pointed at an inanimate target.

But the thought of shooting a living person?

Everything in her rebelled at the idea.

Teagan was a nurturer. Someone who wanted to take care of people and animals.

She never wanted to take a life or to hurt others.

She rubbed her finger along the side of the metal barrel and tried to envision herself having the strength to do whatever was necessary. Not to protect herself.

But to protect her baby.

Her heart pounded harder.

She pressed her eyes closed.

She knew she would do it if she had to.

In the meantime, she lifted a prayer for Hudson and Mateo's safety.

The two of them had no idea what they were walking into at that cabin. Nor did Teagan.

She knew that both men were trained and capable. But sometimes even the most trained and capable people died.

Like her dad.

Teagan still remembered getting the news that he'd died in an accident when she'd been twelve.

Things like that weren't supposed to happen. But they did.

Refocusing on her surroundings, she pushed herself up slightly and glanced around.

As she did, something in the distance caught her eye.

Movement.

Was that a man?

Her lungs froze.

She continued watching, waiting for confirmation that someone was out there.

Praying that she was wrong.

Then she saw the movement again.

Her heart felt as if it had stopped.

Someone *was* out there.

If she had to guess, it was one of Farino's men.

She grabbed the cell phone from the glovebox. With trembling hands, she hit a button and stared at the screen.

Her stomach dropped.

Hudson was right. There was no service out here.

Her pulse thudded in her ears.

Shoving the phone into her back pocket, she gripped the gun.

She needed to make some fast decisions.

Some *gut-wrenching* decisions.

Teagan knew without a doubt that she was going to need a supernatural strength to get through this.

TWENTY-FOUR

"WHAT DO YOU THINK?" Hudson asked Mateo as they crouched behind some bushes, just out of sight of the cabin.

As Mateo stared at the moderately sized chalet, his jaw flexed. "The place looks empty, but we're going to need to get closer."

"I agree. You go left. I'll go right."

They split, remaining low as they approached the house.

Everything around them was quiet as they crept forward.

Hudson paused by the driveway and glanced down.

The tire prints there looked fresh.

Someone had been here recently.

Angela?

That's what they needed to find out.

Hudson headed toward a window. Reaching it, he slowly rose and peered inside.

The living room came into view.

No one was visible.

But that didn't mean this place was empty.

He glanced at Mateo, who pointed to the opposite side to indicate he was going to keep searching the perimeter.

Hudson continued to creep around the edge of the cabin, peering in windows.

But he saw nothing and no one.

A moment later, he and Mateo met at the front door and nodded at each other in silent communication. They each flanked one side before Hudson twisted the knob.

It was locked.

Mateo grabbed a kit from his pocket and picked the lock with expert precision.

Carefully, they pushed the door open. Sometimes the element of quiet surprise was better than a sudden outburst.

An empty house stared back at them.

Hudson slipped inside, tension between his shoulders as he anticipated whatever trouble he might find here.

As the man in the distance crept closer, Teagan slid across the car seat to the opposite side of the vehicle.

Quietly, she opened her door, careful not to make any sounds.

Then she slipped outside.

If she stayed in the car, she'd be a sitting duck.

She had no doubt this guy would find the vehicle anytime now.

She only hoped she could remain quiet and not draw any attention to herself.

Remaining low, she crept in the opposite direction. The gun remained in her hand just in case she needed to use it.

She prayed she didn't.

Instead, she tried to use the cover of trees and bushes to remain out of sight.

She was aware that another guard could also be out in these woods.

What if someone else was scouring the other side of the forest?

Teagan didn't want to be taken by surprise.

A tremble raked through her at the thought.

She hadn't come this far to be captured.

She had to stay positive. To focus on keeping out of sight. She could do this.

At any minute, Hudson and Mateo should return. If things went south, they'd be nearby to help.

Her lungs remained tight as she continued to creep forward. She had to be careful. Stepping on a stick or stumbling on a rock would only draw attention to her.

Such a small act could end up costing her life.

Finally, Teagan spotted a boulder in the distance. Moving quickly, she ducked behind it and sucked in several deep breaths as she tried to get her fear under control.

She'd done it. She'd gotten this far.

Gripping the gun, she straightened enough to peer over the top of the boulder. She hoped to catch a glimpse of the man again.

But only woods stared back at her.

The man was gone.

Her heart pumped harder.

Where was he?

Even worse—what if he was closer than she imagined?

CHAPTER
TWENTY-FIVE

CAREFULLY, Hudson stepped into the cabin, his gun drawn—just in case anyone tried to surprise them.

Mateo slipped in behind him and headed up a set of stairs to what looked like a loft area.

The inside was nice and felt surprisingly cool. Almost like someone had been here and had run the AC. Maybe they left it on all the time. But he doubted it.

Pictures of the Farinos rested on a table near the wall, each photo displaying a smiling, happy family. The images defied the true heart of the family—evil and vile.

He continued through the kitchen, headed toward a door beyond it.

Carefully, he nudged it open.

A bedroom stared back.

With no one in sight, he made his way inside, checking every corner, around the dresser, and under the bed.

No one was here.

But the cover was rumpled, almost like someone had been sitting on it.

Tension crawled up his spine.

Another indication someone might have been here recently.

Had someone known they were coming? Were there cameras set up somewhere—cameras neither he nor Mateo had seen?

He didn't like the thought, but it was a possibility.

His muscles still taut, he went back to the living room just as Mateo came downstairs from the loft.

As images of Teagan and Ricky being alone here together began to flash in his mind, he pressed his eyes closed, trying to shut them out.

Instead, he turned back to Mateo. "Anything?"

Mateo put his gun back into the holster. "No, it's clear."

Hudson glanced around again. "Something about this whole situation feels off, doesn't it?"

"I was thinking the same thing." Mateo put his hands on his hips as he glanced around also.

Hudson's gaze stopped at a box that had been tucked away on the corner of the kitchen counter.

Out of curiosity, he walked toward it.

"Hudson?" Mateo muttered.

"Yeah?"

"I think that might be a camera tucked up there by that deer head."

"A camera?" He glanced back and saw the device Mateo was talking about.

Was someone monitoring this property?

He paused by the box. Using the barrel of his gun, he nudged the sides open.

His breath caught at what he saw.

"Mateo, we've got to get out of here." He quickly backed away.

"What's going on?"

"There's a bomb in here."

Teagan could hardly breathe. It didn't matter what she did or what she told herself, the tension in her chest wouldn't loosen.

Where had the man gone?

She scanned the woods again, but she still didn't see him.

He hadn't disappeared into thin air.

He was here *somewhere*.

She just needed to wait. The worst thing she could do right now was to have a knee-jerk reaction.

She held her breath as the seconds ticked past.

Finally, a stick cracked in the distance.

She jerked her gaze toward the sound, peering carefully around the boulder.

It was the man.

He'd found the car.

Her heart pounded harder as she watched, waiting for his next move.

He held a gun, raised as if ready to fire, and peered in the windows.

Then he snatched a radio from his belt and muttered something into it. Teagan couldn't make out the words.

She continued to watch as the man circled the vehicle, his steps slow and purposeful.

He wore all black and carried a large gun—she didn't know what kind, only that it looked dangerous. The man was tall, and his broad shoulders made him appear strong.

She didn't think she'd seen him before.

But the Farinos had so many people on their payroll that it wasn't a surprise she didn't recognize him.

He glanced around as if looking for someone— maybe as if looking for her.

As he did, Teagan ducked behind the boulder again, afraid he'd seen her.

Then she waited.

The only sound she heard was her heart pounding in her ears and the gentle scrape of the leaves brushing against each other with the strengthening breeze.

What was the man doing? Had he seen her? Was he coming closer?

Teagan forced herself not to move but to wait.

Then she heard a grunt.

After several seconds passed, she ventured to peer over the rock again.

The man had bent over beside the car.

When he rose again, he lifted his gun.

She sucked in a breath as he fired.

At the tires.

All four of them.

He was making sure they couldn't get away, wasn't he?

When he finished, he picked up his radio again and muttered something into it.

The next instant, another sound filled the air.

An explosion.

A cry caught in her throat.

That had come from the top of the hill . . . where the cabin was located.

Hudson . . .

Was he okay?

TWENTY-SIX

HUDSON HIT the ground as the explosion sounded behind him. Warmth from the flames made his skin feel on fire.

He quickly checked himself over.

He was okay.

Looking for Mateo, he glanced around.

His colleague lay on the ground beside him—mere feet outside the cabin.

Hudson's lungs froze. "Mateo?"

At the sound of his voice, Mateo pushed himself up on his elbows. He appeared dazed but otherwise okay.

Thank God.

Hudson's gaze swerved back to the house.

Flames engulfed the structure.

That had been a trap. Somehow, the Farinos had realized the people helping Teagan might come here, and they'd set this up. They'd installed that camera so they could time everything down to the second.

They must have assumed Teagan wouldn't be with them.

Because they didn't appear to want her to die.

But maybe they did.

Hudson would figure that out later.

He only knew if they'd discovered that bomb one minute later, he and Mateo would both be toast right now.

He pulled himself to his feet.

Right before the explosion, he'd heard gunshots.

All he could think about was Teagan.

He took a step toward the woods, ready to sprint back to the car.

He had to know if she was okay.

"We've got to get to Teagan," he muttered, still pulling in shallow breaths.

Mateo's jaw hardened as he stepped toward him. "Let's go. But we need to approach carefully—just in case."

Hudson's gut clenched. He knew what that meant.

Just in case *someone* was nearby. Near Teagan.

He and Mateo couldn't tip their hands.

Every part of him wanted to race through the woods as quickly as possible to make sure Teagan was okay. But that wouldn't be wise.

They needed to be very careful.

One wrong move could mean death.

Teagan realized she was holding her breath and slowly released the air from her lungs. She forced herself to swallow back the cry wanting to escape every time she thought about Hudson. When she thought about him lying on the ground harmed and in pain . . . or worse.

Everything she'd done—that she'd sacrificed—had been to keep him safe.

Now it had come down to this?

Her hand splayed over her stomach.

Even if that was the case, Teagan had someone else to protect now.

That didn't stop the warm tears springing to her eyes.

She would have time to mourn later. Right now, she needed to figure out how to get out of here without being caught.

She was in the middle of nowhere. Without a car or cell phone reception or money. She didn't even have water. She'd already drank the bottle she had in the car.

Another cry of despair tried to bubble up inside her.

Think, Teagan. Think. You can do this. You're strong. Capable. A fighter.

She glanced over the boulder again and saw the man was still there. He muttered something into his radio again, something Teagan couldn't make out.

But it seemed clear he wasn't the only one out here.

Teagan watched for what he would do next. Maybe that should determine her decision.

Her throat felt painfully dry as she waited.

Finally, the man stepped away from the car and headed back in the direction he'd come from.

Was he going to check out the carnage of the cabin? To see what damage had been done?

Her heart pounded harder at the thought.

It was too early to say for sure.

But if that was the case, maybe Teagan could run as soon as he was out of sight.

For now, Teagan waited and watched.

Finally, the man disappeared behind some trees.

But just as Teagan rose to run, movement sounded.

Not from the man who'd just left.

But from the opposite direction.

Cold fear crept up her spine.

What if the person this guy was working with had found her?

CHAPTER
TWENTY-SEVEN

HUDSON HURRIED THROUGH THE WOODS, moving as fast as he could while still being careful.

He had to put his eyes on Teagan. Had to know she was okay.

Behind him, flames continued to climb from the cabin.

Someone had been watching this location. Waiting for them to go inside. The bomb hadn't been on a timer. Hudson was certain of it.

That meant he needed to be even more careful as he walked through these woods.

There might be more cameras set up.

Someone could be out here waiting to surprise them again.

He shoved a tree limb out of the way as he continued forward.

He shouldn't have brought Teagan here. He should have known better.

This had all been for nothing.

He wound between trees, heading down the mountain.

As he did, he scanned his surroundings.

He couldn't see the car yet. It should be just over the next ridge.

Movement in the distance drew his gaze.

He grabbed Mateo's arm and pulled him behind a tree.

They paused and watched as a man wearing all black walked toward the cabin.

Hudson didn't think the man had seen them.

And Teagan wasn't with him.

Hudson counted that as a good sign.

They waited until the man had passed before moving again.

"One of Farino's guys?" Mateo whispered as he peered at him.

"That's my best guess."

Fire burned through Hudson's blood at the thought of it. He'd like nothing more than to take this guy down.

But he kept moving forward.

He had to get to Teagan.

Finally, he spotted the car in the distance.

From here, the vehicle appeared untouched.

Moving more quickly, Hudson reached it and peered inside.

It was empty.

Teagan was gone.

His heart rate accelerated even more.

Had that guy done something to Teagan?

His jaw clenched.

He wouldn't be able to live with himself if that was what had happened.

That's when he looked down and saw the tires had been shot out.

***

Teagan heard more movement in the distance.

But she didn't dare move.

Not until she knew who was making the sounds.

She waited, her fingers digging into the boulder in front of her.

The sun was sinking in the sky now, and darkness was beginning to fall.

She didn't know if the nighttime scared her or provided comfort. At least, it helped conceal her. But the growing shadows also helped conceal anyone following her.

When she heard a pause and things got quiet, she dared to lift her head.

The breath left her lungs when she saw Hudson standing near the car examining it.

Based on the slump of his shoulders, he'd been thinking of worst-case scenarios also.

More than anything, Teagan wanted to wipe that haunted look from his face.

She rose and waved her hand, not wanting to risk yelling.

"Over here," she whispered as loudly as she could.

Hudson glanced up, his relief visible. His shoulders slanted, and his head fell back slightly. But only for a moment.

The next instant, he ran toward her. He reached her and pulled her into a hug. "Teagan . . . I'm glad you're okay."

"Me too. The guy who shot out your tires, he disappeared back up the mountain. I thought you were . . ." She couldn't finish her sentence as a sob stuck in her throat.

"No, we're fine. But it was close. We need to get you out of here."

She glanced over and noticed that Mateo remained near the car, still checking it out and giving them some space.

At least, they were both okay.

She was grateful beyond words for that.

A shout sounded in the distance.

Teagan saw two men appear at the crest of the hill.

What were they going to do now?

TWENTY-EIGHT

HUDSON PULLED Teagan down below the boulder and peered around the side.

Based on where the men were standing, they couldn't have seen him and Teagan yet.

Only Mateo.

Mateo ducked behind a tree, offered a subtle nod to Hudson. Neither had to say anything to know what the other was thinking.

Mateo would lead these guys away and create a diversion. While he did that, Hudson would get Teagan to safety. She was their first priority right now.

Mateo took off into a run in the opposite direction.

Hudson watched as the two men chased after him.

Only when they were out of sight did Hudson grab her hand. "We've got to get out of here."

"What about Mateo?"

"He'll be fine. Let's go. The more distance we have between them and us the better."

Teagan didn't ask any more questions. She simply stayed behind him as he led her through the woods. Led her away from the cabin. Away from Mateo.

As he did, the wind kicked up. Thunder rumbled in the distance.

A storm was coming.

A storm that might help give them cover or might slow them down.

He wasn't sure which at this point. Maybe both.

All the while, Hudson kept his eyes open for anyone else who might be out here looking for them.

The best thing they could do right now was to keep moving.

His team knew what was going on. They would come and help.

But right now, movement meant life.

They climbed the mountainside and over rocks and across trees fallen in their path. They pushed through thick underbrush and climbed boulders.

Big, fat drops of rain began to fall.

Lightning flashed in the sky.

The wind blew debris into them.

Finally, after they'd covered at least two miles, Hudson paused and glanced at Teagan.

Surprise washed through him when he saw how pale she looked. How labored her breathing sounded.

Concern ricocheted through him.

He stepped closer. "Are you okay?"

She nodded but continued to draw in deep breaths, her hand going over her abdomen as if she were cramping up again. Rain pelted them, and the sharp wind made everything feel cool—almost chilly—despite the otherwise warm weather.

"Can you keep moving?" Hudson could stop here, but there was nowhere for them to hunker down. No roads for the rescue team. No shelter from the storm.

"I'll be fine." But her voice sounded raspy as she said the words.

Hudson glanced around.

They needed to get somewhere secure. Then Teagan needed to lie down. Maybe this had all been too much for her.

His thoughts also went to Mateo. What he'd told Teagan was true. Mateo could handle those two men.

But what if more guys showed up?

This whole situation was precarious.

And one wrong move could mean death.

Quickly, Teagan removed her hand from over her abdomen. She hadn't meant to place it there. But the instinct had seemed natural, a way of protecting the baby inside her.

She'd looked into the mirror just this morning and had noticed that her belly was growing—just this week alone, it seemed. Her clothes were beginning to feel a little tight also.

How long would it be before she could no longer

hide the life growing inside her? Baggy shirts might work for a while, but then what?

She couldn't worry about that right now.

She pulled herself together.

Teagan knew she and Hudson had to keep moving. Doing anything else was not an option.

"I'm okay." She raised her head, trying to appear stronger than she felt.

Hudson looked at her, not hiding his concern.

"Let's keep going." Even though Teagan tried to sound certain as she said the words, she felt herself getting weak. Felt her energy waning.

But she'd rest later—once she knew they were safe.

"We'll go a little slower," Hudson said. "But if you need to stop, tell me."

That was the one thing Teagan had always loved about Hudson. He was so patient.

Ricky had always had a quick temper, and Teagan felt like she was walking on eggshells around him. It wasn't that he was abusive. His emotions were just volatile at times.

With another lingering glance at her, Hudson hesitantly began leading Teagan through the woods again. But each step felt heavy.

How much longer would she make it?

Was she putting her baby at risk by continuing to walk?

Maybe she should just tell Hudson what was going on. Why was she keeping all these secrets?

Somehow, it felt safer for no one to know.

But how would Hudson knowing about her condition be risky?

It probably wouldn't be.

Except for her heart.

Maybe Teagan was overthinking this. But she felt certain Hudson would be hurt when he heard the news.

Or maybe that thought was ridiculous. Hudson probably didn't have any feelings for her anymore. After all, he'd believed she was dead for two years. A lot could have changed.

She continued forward, her steps slower.

But as soon as she heard a stick crack behind her, all of those worries disappeared—replaced by even more terrifying ones.

CHAPTER
TWENTY-NINE

HUDSON HEARD the stick snap and froze. He pulled Teagan behind a tree and waited.

Had those men found them?

He prayed that wasn't the case.

He waited a moment before peering out.

Then he saw it.

A deer.

The animal looked just as startled to see them as they did to see it.

Hudson let out a little breath. "It's okay. It's just a doe."

Teagan seemed to slouch with relief. "I thought for sure they'd found us."

That's what Hudson had worried about also.

She glanced back in the direction they'd come from. "How far do you think we've gone now?"

He glanced at his watch that recorded his steps. "Three and a half miles."

"How much farther?"

"Do you need to stop?" He studied her face.

She opened her mouth as if to say something, but she shut it again and shook her head. "I'll go however far we need to."

"It's getting dark. We're going to need to find some shelter soon. I'm looking for a good place where we can stay put. A couple guys from the extraction finished already. They're on their way here to help."

"Do you really think Mateo is okay?" She stared at him, her eyes reminding him of that doe he'd just seen.

"He's a smart guy. And he's fast. I think he'll be fine."

Teagan nodded, but the motion looked strained and heavy.

Quickly, Hudson pulled her into a hug. "We're going to get through this."

To his surprise, Teagan melted against him. She remained in his arms several moments as if she gained some type of strength from his touch.

That fact didn't go unnoticed by him. A thrill rushed through him as he realized she was comfortable enough with him to rest in his embrace.

He'd missed this so much.

But they didn't have time to stay here forever.

Hudson stepped back and took her hand, instantly missing the warmth of her body. "We should get moving."

Teagan nodded and drew in a shaky breath.

Then they started through the woods again.

Just when Teagan thought she couldn't take another step, Hudson paused and pointed to something in the distance.

"Do you see that?" he asked.

"See what?"

"It's an old shack."

Her eyes lit when she saw the structure.

The rustic wood sides of the building nearly blended into the woods, and the roof had trees growing on top. Unless someone was looking closely, they might not even notice the place. She certainly hadn't.

"I'm going to check out the inside," Hudson said. "I need to see if it's somewhere we can hunker down until the storm passes. I can also drop my team a pin to let them know where we are."

Teagan shuddered at the thought of going inside that place. At the thought of the bugs and snakes that had probably taken up residence there.

But Hudson would be with her, and she knew he wouldn't let anything happen to her.

As she waited outside, she scanned everything around her, halfway expecting the worst. Halfway expecting someone else to appear.

Instead, Hudson stepped out of the cabin and motioned toward her. "This should work. It's not ideal, but the place isn't as bad as it looks on the outside either."

She was going to have to trust him on that.

He led her inside, and, using a flashlight he'd brought, he shone the beam around the space.

He was right. The place wasn't as bad as she'd thought.

A cot stretched in the corner. A small table with two chairs were across from the cot. Some buckets and bowls had been set up on a plywood counter near the door.

And the knobby wood floor was surprisingly clean.

"Someone probably uses this place when they come out here hunting," Hudson explained, holding onto her elbow. "It'll be a good spot to lie low for a little while. Are you okay with it?"

Just as he asked the question, everything around Teagan began to spin. Her vision blurred until she felt herself wobble.

Hudson caught her and lowered her onto the cot.

"Teagan? Teagan, are you okay?" He leaned closer.

She pressed her eyes shut and fought the wave of nausea and light-headedness that consumed her.

AS THUNDER RUMBLED across the sky, Teagan nearly jumped into Hudson's arms.

He wasn't complaining. Instead, Hudson pulled her close until her head rested on his chest.

For a moment, the two of them together felt like old times. Like nothing had changed.

But everything had.

Everything but Hudson's feelings.

They'd always been there. He hadn't even dated anyone since Teagan's supposed death. Not really. Just a few one-offs here and there.

But no one had compared to Teagan.

No one ever would.

Hudson wished he had more to offer her here at this cabin. Maybe some water or food.

But the cabinets were empty.

Hopefully, his team would be here soon. Service was spotty, but he hoped they'd gotten his pinned location.

As the thunder faded, Teagan drew back.

But as she glanced up, her eyes met his. Their gazes locked onto one another, something magnetic seeming to pass between them.

Against his better instincts, Hudson reached for her. His hand cupped her jaw.

He gently traced the outline of her ear, her cheek, her lips.

She closed her eyes and leaned into his touch. "Oh, Hudson . . ."

Hearing his name whispered from her lips was all the affirmation Hudson needed. As he leaned closer, Teagan wrapped her arms around his neck.

Their lips met in an explosive kiss. One that seemed to try to make up for all the time they'd been apart. For all the damage that had been done.

All the hurt was forgotten.

For a moment, at least.

Teagan raked her fingers through the hair at the nape of his neck as they clung to each other.

Then just as abruptly, she pulled away.

She scrambled back as if she wasn't sure what she'd done.

Her eyes widened with confusion . . . or maybe regret.

Hudson reeled at her sudden withdrawal.

He touched his lips, trying to confirm that kiss had just happened and hadn't just been a figment of his imagination.

It wasn't.

Their kiss had been real. Better than he'd ever dreamed.

So, why did Teagan look so scared right now?

She dragged her gaze up to meet his. "Hudson, there's something I need to tell you."

"Go ahead."

She opened her mouth to speak. But, before any words emerged, she scrambled to her feet and dashed across the room to a bucket in the distance.

Leaning over it, she vomited.

***

Teagan felt Hudson behind her, placing a hand on her back as she leaned over the bucket.

"Are you okay?" Concern laced his voice.

Her pulse raced as she straightened, using her shirt to wipe her mouth.

She hadn't expected that. The nausea had hit her again. She'd been powerless to stop the reflex.

Hudson helped her to her feet, and as she looked into his eyes, her resolve crumbled.

She couldn't do this. Couldn't tell him the truth.

Yet she had to.

She cared about him too much to keep this secret from him any longer.

"Hudson . . ." She swallowed hard, trying to scrounge every ounce of courage inside her. "I don't know how to say this, but . . . I'm pregnant."

His eyebrows shot up so fast they nearly flew off his face, and he took a step back. "You're what?"

Her throat burned as she swallowed. "I'm pregnant. I know I should have told you sooner, but—"

He looked away, raking a hand through his hair in disbelief. Finally, he looked back at her, confusion in his gaze. "You're . . . pregnant?"

"I know this comes as a shock, but—"

"Why didn't you tell me this from the beginning?"

Apprehension lodged in her chest. "I was going to, but . . ."

"But what?"

That seemed like a good question right now.

She opened her mouth and then shut it again.

Suddenly, all her excuses seemed worthless and inadequate.

She swallowed hard before saying, "You're the first person I've told. I don't want people to know."

Hudson's gaze latched onto hers, and she saw the realizations clicking in place in his mind. "*That's* why the Farinos want you so badly, isn't it? Because you're carrying Ricky's baby."

Teagan nodded, her hand going over her stomach again, but this time without any hesitation or regret. "Yes. That's why. I can't let my child be a part of that family."

Hudson's gaze seemed to harden. "Did Ricky know?"

"I only found out a couple of weeks ago. I tried to

hide all the evidence so no one would find out. But Lucia figured it out. I'm not sure how."

"The Farinos have a way of finding out everything, don't they?" He narrowed his gaze as if the thought disgusted him.

"Hudson . . ." Teagan reached for him, but he pulled back.

An ache filled her chest. But she didn't blame him for his reaction. What had she expected?

"I'm sorry." She stepped back and tucked her arms across her chest. "I don't know what else to say."

He rubbed a hand over his face before turning away again. Then he lifted his head and shook it, his shoulders tight.

"You're carrying Ricky's baby." Agony filled his voice.

Teagan knew it took a special man to embrace another man's baby.

Was Hudson up for the task?

He wasn't offering to be. Their relationship wasn't even really a relationship anymore. It was just a kiss.

But Teagan had felt so much hope in that moment.

Before they could talk about it anymore, noises sounded outside.

Someone was here, she realized.

The question was . . . was it Hudson's team?

Or the Farinos?

THIRTY-ONE

HUDSON DREW his gun and pushed himself in front of Teagan.

It was too late to hide—not that there was anywhere to do so inside this tiny cabin.

He'd heard at least three sets of boots moving outside.

He and Teagan were surrounded.

"Hudson, it's me," a deep voice said. "Mateo."

Hudson's shoulders softened, and he lowered his gun.

His team was here.

Thank goodness.

Because he needed to get Teagan somewhere safe . . . especially now that he knew about her condition.

Still cautious, he opened the door.

Sure enough, his colleagues stood on the other side, guns in hand and shoulders braced as they watched for trouble.

"Everybody okay?" Mateo asked.

"Now we are," Hudson said. "Can you get us out of here?"

"Absolutely. Let's go." He looped his hand in the air and motioned for them to follow.

Hudson took Teagan's hand and led her outside.

Knowing that she was pregnant only made everything more urgent. Only made Hudson's quest to keep her safe more important.

But . . . pregnant? This was going to take some time to comprehend.

It changed everything.

Or did it?

He followed his team down a pathway. He assumed a vehicle was waiting nearby.

Hudson turned to Mateo. "You got away from them?"

Hudson helped Teagan down a particularly slippery part of the trail as he waited for an answer.

Between the darkness, their exhaustion, and the recent rain, the walk was treacherous.

"It took longer than I thought it would," Mateo said. "There were a couple of moments when things got pretty dicey. But I managed to lose them. These guys aren't playing around."

Hudson's jaw tightened. "You're right. They're not. We're lucky we're all walking away from this in one piece."

That fact only reminded Hudson that he needed to get Teagan back to the ranch where she could be safe.

Bringing her here had been a mistake.

They reached the end of the path, and a black Hummer came into view.

He ushered Teagan into the backseat before slipping in behind her.

As soon as everyone was inside and the door closed, the driver took off.

They would fly back to Arizona, and then he would tuck Teagan away . . . forever if that was what he had to do.

***

By the time Teagan arrived back at the ranch, she nearly felt beside herself.

That had been close. Too close.

For some reason, she now had a nagging worry that maybe her baby wasn't okay.

She'd been going off instinct this whole time. She'd felt fine up until now other than the occasional nausea.

Maybe the stress of the situation had finally gotten to her.

Her hand remained on her stomach for almost the entire flight. She had fallen asleep on the plane and had woken up with it still over her stomach.

Hudson remained distant. No doubt, he was still processing everything—as anyone would in his shoes.

Maybe the tension between them wouldn't hurt so much if they hadn't shared that kiss only moments before Teagan had revealed her secret. For a few precious moments, things had felt the way they'd used to between them.

She only wished it had lasted longer.

As soon as they arrived back at the ranch, Charlie met her outside. It was morning now, and lemonade-colored sunlight filtered over the mountain range in the distance.

It would have been a sight to admire . . . if she didn't have so many other things on her mind.

"We have a doctor here who can check you out," Charlie told her.

Clearly, Hudson had updated his boss.

Teagan nodded, relieved to have medical care available.

A few minutes later, she was ushered into a room at the back of the building.

A small exam room. Teagan hadn't even known this was here.

But it made sense, considering how far out they were on the ranch.

A thirty-something woman with wavy auburn hair, who wore a lab coat and stethoscope, waited inside.

She offered a bright smile. "Hi there. I'm Dr. Cossette, and I'd like to check you and the baby out just to make sure everything is okay."

Teagan glanced back one more time and saw Hudson standing several feet away. She couldn't read the look on his face.

Part of her wanted someone in the room with her to hold her hand.

But she didn't think that Hudson was that person.

Not right now, at least.

Something about that thought brought her a disheartening disappointment.

Averting her gaze, she closed the door to get ready for her exam.

HUDSON NEARLY COLLAPSED into a chair in the mess hall.

No one else was in here yet. But in an hour or so, this place would probably be full as the lunch crowd headed this way.

He ran a hand through his hair, feeling a headache coming.

This was all almost too much for him to process. Teagan was not only alive, but she was pregnant, and a deadly crime family would do anything to get her back in their possession.

Maybe he still hadn't even comprehended the fact she was still alive.

Charlie stepped into the room and pulled out the seat across from him.

"How are you doing?" She studied his face as if she honestly wanted to know.

He shrugged. "I'm not sure."

Hudson's words were true. He still didn't know.

He only knew that, as he'd watched Teagan sleeping on the plane, something had stirred inside him. She was the woman he'd dreamed about spending the rest of his life with.

Now she was back . . . yet she still felt so far away.

"You still love her, don't you?" Charlie continued to study his face, her discerning eyes watching every detail of his reaction.

Did he? Hudson couldn't even pretend like he didn't know the answer.

"I don't think I ever stopped loving Teagan," he finally said. "But her being pregnant changes everything."

Charlie tilted her head. "How?"

Hudson gave her a look. Did she really have to ask that? "She's carrying another man's baby. I assumed she was unhappily married or married in name only. Not that . . ." How did he even finish? "That she'd get pregnant."

"So, the baby changes everything? Because the baby's not yours?" She tilted her head as she waited for his answer.

He couldn't be sure, but there almost seemed to be something deeper in her voice, a catch he hadn't expected to hear.

As quickly as he heard the emotion, it was gone.

"I don't know. I don't know anything anymore." Hudson's headache began pulsing harder.

"That baby isn't all Ricky. It's part Teagan and all the

wonderful qualities she possesses. She's going to need support."

Hudson pressed his eyes closed. "I'm not sure if I'm meant to be the one to give that to her. Besides, she's going to start a new life in Florida. Meanwhile, I work here in Arizona."

"And . . . ?"

"It's really too soon to talk about this anyway. For the past two years, I thought Teagan was dead."

"And now you're getting a second chance." Charlie's voice sounded surprisingly gentle. "That's an amazing opportunity."

He dragged his gaze up to meet hers. "Just because it's an amazing opportunity doesn't mean it's going to work out."

"That doesn't mean that it won't either. Process what's going on. But just know that more than anything Teagan needs someone here for her right now. You don't want to make any decisions that you're going to regret further down the road."

Charlie's words settled on him.

She was right.

Hudson had some decisions to make.

And time wasn't on his side.

"Everything looks great." Dr. Cossette draped her stethoscope around her neck as she addressed Teagan.

Teagan sat up on the examination table, relief filling her.

"But you need to take it easy," the doctor continued. "All the stress you've been under isn't good for you or the baby."

Teagan rubbed her belly. "I know. I'm doing my best."

"I can only imagine what it's like to be in your situation." Dr. Cossette took a step back and leaned against the wall, all her attention on Teagan. "But the baby has a nice strong heartbeat, and your blood pressure is good. I'd like to see you once a month, at least while you're here. Once you're settled in a new location, I can recommend a good OB/GYN for you."

"I'd appreciate that." For some reason, Dr. Cossette's words caused a shot of fear to rush through Teagan.

Teagan knew she'd be starting over in a new place with a new identity.

That also meant she'd be all alone at her appointments. Alone for the birth of her baby. Alone during those first few weeks with a newborn, unsure exactly what to do.

What if she needed help? What if something went wrong? How would she handle being alone and not getting any sleep?

She set those thoughts aside for a moment.

Teagan would get through it. She had no other choice.

But this wasn't the way she'd seen her life going.

No, she was supposed to work her job as a travel

writer. Marry Hudson. Settle down in a nice house in the country—but only after exploring the world for a while. And then they would have kids together. Four or five. They both wanted a big family.

She was an adult. She couldn't hold onto regrets or fears. She couldn't change the past. So, she'd have to make do with what she had.

The doctor's hand cupped her shoulder. "You take care of yourself and that baby, understand?"

Teagan nodded as she slid down from the table. "I understand."

Keeping her baby safe had become her primary mission in life.

THIRTY-THREE

HUDSON STOOD AS SOON as he saw Teagan emerge from the exam room.

He started to speak, but nothing left his lips. His words seemed to lodge in his throat as he paused in front of Teagan.

"Well?" He studied her face, trying to read if she'd just gotten good or bad news.

"The baby and I are doing just fine." Teagan offered him a reassuring nod. "Thanks for rushing to get me back here."

He stared at her a moment, realizing once again just how beautiful she was. He now understood the glow she had about her. It had been a *pregnancy* glow.

He'd imagined many times what it would be like for Teagan to carry his baby. He'd imagined feeling the baby kick. The joy of watching her belly grow.

But never in his imagination had it been like this.

He cleared his throat, trying to push those thoughts aside. "You should probably get some rest."

She opened her mouth as if she wanted to argue, but she finally nodded. "I probably should."

"I can walk you back to your cabana."

Silently, they fell into step beside each other.

"Anything on Angela?" she finally asked.

He shook his head. "No, I'm sorry. I wish I had more to tell you."

"Does that mean that you guys have given up on the investigation?" She paused in the middle of the dusty walkway and looked up at him.

"No, not at all. We hit a roadblock, and now we're coming up with a new plan."

She nodded and glanced away. "Thank you."

He stared at her another moment. He wanted to say so much. Yet he wasn't certain where to start.

I care about you. I want to be the man you deserve. I don't want to blow this, but I need to figure things out.

None of those words left his lips.

Instead, Hudson paused outside Teagan's cabana.

She stopped in the doorway and turned to him, an unreadable expression in her gaze. "I'll talk to you later."

For some reason, her words almost sounded like a goodbye.

Teagan lay in bed, but she couldn't sleep.

How could she rest knowing her friend was out there and possibly suffering? The answer was easy.

She couldn't.

The need to take care of people collided with the need to protect herself. Still, she also knew she needed to take care of herself in order to take care of her baby.

But her friend was also in danger.

The clashing thoughts caused tension to spread through her.

Tension was *exactly* what she didn't need. Dr. Cossette had told her to stay away from that kind of stress.

Teagan pressed her eyes closed.

There had to be *something* she could do.

Teagan searched her thoughts for a solution.

As she lay there, an idea hit her, and she sat up.

It was probably a longshot. Probably nothing would come of it.

But maybe it would provide an answer.

First, she had to find Hudson.

She scrambled out of bed and stepped into the midmorning heat. She squinted against the bright sunlight as she scanned the area around her.

Various people wandered around the ranch.

But no Hudson.

Hurrying, she rushed into the mess hall and surveyed everyone around her.

As soon as Hudson saw her, he stood from the table where he'd been eating breakfast.

He quickly strode across the room to meet her. "Is everything okay?"

"I have an idea. A way that we might find answers."

He narrowed his gaze. "What's that?"

"Before I escaped, I set up a secret email account."

Hudson glanced around before taking her elbow and leading her away from anyone who might be listening. "Secret email?"

Teagan nodded, her thoughts still racing and adrenaline pumping through her. "I tried to set it up so it couldn't be traced back to me."

"If it was on your computer, then it *could* be traced back to you."

"I set it up on a work computer at the shelter. I figured my in-laws wouldn't be able to find it there. I didn't use any of my real information so it couldn't be traced back to me."

He stared at her another moment. "Why did you set that up?"

"I thought, at one point, that maybe I could try to contact you that way."

"Okay, but . . ." He shook his head, not bothering to hide his confusion. "I'm still not sure how that's going to help you now."

"What if the Farinos found out about it? What if they emailed me, knowing it was a way to reach me?"

He reached for her, squeezing her arm as if trying to bring her back down to reality. "I really doubt your former in-laws are going to email you anything."

A frown tugged at her lips. "There's got to be a way to check without being traced."

Hudson pressed his lips together. "It's unlikely— and it's too risky. The Farinos would be monitoring that email if they knew about it."

"But think about it," Teagan continued, undeterred. "Why did they grab Angela? To get to me. But I disappeared. They have to think of a way to send me a message. They can't just broadcast it over the news. What better way than by email?"

"They have to know the FBI is monitoring all their messages."

She crossed her arms. "All the ones the FBI knows about. If I can set up a secret email account, think of what they can do. I'm sure they have ways to send emails without being traced. Which is why it would be ideal if they sent a message to my secret email account."

"You said some guy named Art Lansdown started working at the shelter recently?" Hudson's eyes flickered with thought. "That he seemed suspicious?"

Teagan nodded. "That's right. Maybe he was planted there and saw me setting the account up. It's the only thing that makes sense. Maybe you could try and get some information from him?"

"That would be a problem."

Teagan squinted. "What do you mean?"

"I intended on telling you this earlier, but it slipped my mind with everything going on. I already looked into him. Teagan, he died in a hiking accident last week.

Fell from a cliff, and his body wasn't found until two days later."

She gasped. "What?"

Hudson nodded, his expression stoic. "I didn't want to freak you out."

"That was no accident. They killed him . . ."

Hudson's jaw tightened. "That's what it looks like."

CHAPTER
THIRTY-FOUR

HUDSON TOLD his team what Teagan had told them.

Everyone listened to each new detail.

"It does seem risky to check that email, and it's unlikely we'll discover anything," Charlie said.

Hudson's thoughts continued to race, just as they had ever since Teagan had presented him with this idea. "If Teagan does this, is it even possible for her to look without us signaling to them that she's here? Could they trace the IP address or something?"

"We have ways to disguise that." Charlie took a sip of her coffee. "However, if she does this and she chooses to contact the outside world again, we're going against all the rules we have set up when she came here. I'm not sure we'll be able to support her anymore."

"What?" Hudson wasn't sure he'd heard her correctly.

"It's not that I wouldn't want to," Charlie explained. "But we've already put a lot of time and resources into creating a new life for her. If Teagan is going to continue to be in contact with people from her old life, then our plan isn't going to work."

Hudson's heart beat harder. He couldn't stand that thought. More than anything, he wanted Teagan to be safe.

But, on the other hand, Charlie was right. The team here at Vanishing Ranch had invested a great amount in Teagan's rescue and relocation. If Teagan continued to engage, their plan would be useless.

His heart pounded in his ears.

Hudson knew what he wanted Teagan to do.

He also knew he couldn't make the choice for her, no matter how much he wanted to.

His gaze locked with Charlie's. "What should we do?"

Charlie let out a long breath. "Send Teagan in here. I'll talk to her."

Hudson stood, feeling twenty pounds heavier as he nodded. "Will do."

Charlie tapped her fingers together as she observed Teagan. "We think there's a way we may be able to access your email without anyone tracing your location back here. It's complicated, but our tech guy, Brody, says he can scramble a signal or something. I don't really care to know the details."

Teagan tried not to squirm as she sat in front of Charlie, but her mind wouldn't stop racing through all the consequences and what ifs. "If there's a chance that the Farinos are going to discover Vanishing Ranch and destroy what you're doing here, then I don't want to do it."

She knew one thing: she wasn't a prisoner here like she'd been at the Farino compound. These people wanted to help her.

By the nature of that, Teagan had to have freedom to make her own choices. What she didn't want to do was to put other people at risk or even put this whole entire operation on the line.

Charlie nodded slowly. "I appreciate the fact you're thinking of us. But, believe me, we wouldn't do this if we thought we were going to put anyone here in danger. It just wouldn't be wise."

"Good. I'm glad we're on the same page." Her lungs loosened slightly.

"However, we would be breaking some protocols," Charlie continued. "One of the things you agreed to when you came here for our help was to cut off all communication with the outside world and walk away from your old life. By checking this email account, that's not what we're doing. We already made the exception when you went to try to find your friend."

Teagan nodded. "I know. I'm sorry I didn't keep my

word. I never envisioned the way everything would unfold or that Angela would be in danger. It's made me rethink all my choices."

Charlie leaned forward. "You know better than anyone that the Farinos are bad people. They're not going to stop until they get to you. Even if we're able to rescue Angela, which at this point is iffy, your in-laws will continue to hunt down people you care about. Your old friends from high school. Distant relatives. Anyone you'd want to protect."

An ache formed in Teagan's chest. "I know. But does that mean I just run while all the people I love suffer?"

"I know from what Hudson has told me about you that you're not that type. That you're the kind of person who'd sacrifice yourself in order to make sure the people you love are safe. That's what you did with Hudson, isn't it?"

Tears filled Teagan's eyes again. She had to stop crying. She grabbed a tissue and dabbed her eyes. "I couldn't stand the thought of anything happening to him."

"That's admirable and very extraordinary in today's world. But you need to really think this through and know for sure that this is what you want to do."

"As long as you're sure it's safe . . ." Teagan didn't even have to think about her choice. "I want to see what's in my email, just so I can know if there's anything there that might help Angela."

Charlie stared at her one more moment before

nodding. "Okay then. I'll have my guy set it up. As soon as we know we can safely check it, you can open your email."

HUDSON STOOD behind Teagan and watched as she typed in her login information on the laptop in front of her.

Everything on the laptop was broadcast on a larger screen at the front of the conference room. But he had the urge to remain close to Teagan just in case she needed him.

A moment later, her inbox appeared.

One email was there.

The subject line read: an offer you can't refuse.

Teagan sucked in a breath. "This has to be it."

The sender used a generic email address, a scramble of letters and numbers that made no sense.

No doubt that was purposeful.

"Am I safe to click on it?" Teagan's voice sounded shaky as she asked the question and shifted her gaze to Charlie.

Charlie stood near the larger screen, her arms crossed as she nodded. "Go ahead."

Teagan hesitated only a moment before clicking the message.

As soon as she did, a video began playing.

Angela's face filled the screen.

Angela, who now had a black eye, bloody nose, and a dull gaze.

Teagan gasped at the sight of her.

Despite himself, Hudson placed his hand on Teagan's shoulder.

He knew it was a shock to see her friend in that condition.

"Kat, if you're watching this, they're making me do this video right now. They said that it's your life or mine. They need you to reply to this message. When you do, they'll send you an address and a time. They'll let me go in exchange for you."

Angela paused as if collecting herself. She swallowed hard before continuing.

"If you involve the FBI, the deal is off, and people will die." Angela's gaze flickered as if looking at someone in the background. Then she quickly rushed, "Don't do it, Kat! Don't do it!"

Then the screen went black.

Everyone sat in silence as they processed what they'd just watched.

Angela was clearly in trouble. She was in *a lot* of trouble.

According to the video, the only way she'd ever be

safe was if Kat/Teagan exchanged her life for her friend's.

A storm churned inside Hudson.

If he knew Teagan, he knew exactly what she would want to do.

And he didn't like the answer.

The meeting ended, and Teagan stood to go back to her cabana.

She needed to lie down for a little while.

The image of an injured Angela pleading for her life wouldn't leave Teagan's mind.

Had the Farinos questioned why Teagan was working at the animal shelter? Had they somehow planted something on that computer to trace all the keystrokes just in case she did something like this? Maybe Art had gotten suspicious and told them to search the computer.

The Farinos were the types who'd send someone in after hours to get the information they needed.

That theory was the only thing that made sense.

Teagan wouldn't put it past them to do something like that.

How many other things did they know?

"Teagan! Wait up!"

She turned to see Hudson jogging toward her.

He paused in front of her and studied her face. Then he shifted before saying, "I know that had to be tough to see."

"That would be an understatement."

He shoved his hands into his front pockets. "I want to let you know that everyone in that room is working on a plan to help Angela."

She nodded slowly, almost feeling numb. Just when she thought things couldn't get worse . . . they did. And she hated how powerless that made her feel.

"I appreciate that," she finally said.

"I know it's hard for you to let other people help. But in this case, having an entire support network is only wise."

"Absolutely."

He stepped closer. "And I know what you're thinking. Whatever happens, Teagan . . . you can't trade yourself for Angela."

She nodded slowly, feeling trapped again. Even if she wanted to take matters into her own hands, she was helpless to do so here at the ranch. She was too far away from anything to leave on her own.

That left her at the mercy of the people who'd rescued her.

She cleared her throat and instead asked, "What's next?"

Hudson shifted. "I don't know. All these plane trips . . . they're expensive. We don't have unlimited funding here. The money we have is supposed to go to the women we want to help so they can establish new lives. Of course, we want to help Angela, but there are only so many things we can do for her in this situation. Our main priority is you."

Teagan looked away.

She understood what Hudson was saying. She understood that all these trips and all the travel cost money—money she didn't have to give them. If she thought there was any possibility she could repay them one day, she would.

Everyone here at Vanishing Ranch had already done so much for her, and Teagan had no right to ask them to do even more.

But there had to be *something* she could do.

She just needed to keep thinking.

"I'm going to go lie down." Teagan pointed with her thumb behind her at her cabana.

Hudson's gaze lingered on her a moment longer until he nodded. "That sounds like a good idea. I'm going to go back and continue talking to the team. But I'll give you an update as soon as we know something."

Teagan just prayed that their next update wasn't that Angela was dead.

MONROE PULLED Hudson into his office two hours later. Neither man bothered to sit.

"We just got a return email." Monroe's gaze looked shadowed as if he didn't like any of this. "They want Teagan to meet at the site of an old warehouse outside of Dallas. I checked it out on the satellite. The building is gone, but the parking lot is still there."

"When?"

"Tonight."

Hudson sucked in a breath and crossed his arms. He didn't like the sound of that. "So, what's our plan?"

"In a nutshell? We're going to leave tonight and use Sienna as a decoy. We'll give her a wig in hopes these guys will think she's Teagan, or Kat, as they call her. Then we'll grab Angela and get her to safety."

Hudson processed that a moment. Would that really work? What other choice did they have?

"Using Sienna is a good idea," Hudson said. "You're

not just going to pass this information along to the FBI?"

Monroe rubbed his jaw, and his gaze shifted. "No, not yet. The Farinos could have contacts within the bureau, and we don't want word to get back to the Farinos."

"Makes sense." Hudson shifted, still running through how everything was going to play out. "When are we leaving?"

Monroe glanced at his watch. "In three hours, as soon as it's dark. But we need to keep this under wraps. Teagan doesn't need to know what we're doing. I'd rather tell her after the mission is complete—especially considering her current state."

"I agree." The more they could keep her stress levels down, the better.

"Great. Let's meet at 2100 hours ready to go."

Teagan had gotten a little rest in her cabana, but now she needed to stretch her legs.

She wandered to the place where she was instinctively drawn.

The stable.

She found Bessy and the new foal in their stall.

"You look like you're doing well, Mama," Teagan murmured.

As soon as Bessy saw her, the mare raised her head as if she knew Teagan would soon have a baby also.

Did animals have those kinds of instincts? Teagan didn't know. But she liked that idea.

Mothering came naturally, right? In the animal kingdom it seemed to.

Teagan could handle being a mom.

She would figure it out on her own.

She had no other choice.

Teagan peered over the edge of the stall and watched Jitterbug. The little guy was adorable standing beside his mama.

No matter how scary it might seem right now, a part of her couldn't wait to have her own baby in her arms.

She reached up and rubbed Bessy's face as the animal leaned into her touch.

"You're my inspiration," she whispered to Bessy.

Bessy let out a little snort.

Teagan giggled before rubbing Bessy's face more and murmuring sweet encouragements in the horse's ear.

After a couple of minutes, Bessy let out a puff of air from her nostrils and turned toward Jitterbug.

Teagan smiled and started back toward the mess hall.

But when she reached the stable door, she paused.

Two voices floated in from outside.

"That's right. We're leaving tonight." That voice belonged to Hudson. "Did you hear the plan?"

"Monroe said something to me about it." The other voice clearly belonged to Mateo.

What were they talking about?

"Do you think it will work?" Mateo continued.

"I hope so," Hudson said. "Because we're running out of options and time. Having Sienna there will definitely help."

"What does Teagan think?"

"Monroe said not to tell her."

Teagan's breath caught as she continued to listen.

"Probably a good idea. She needs to keep her stress level down."

"I think so too. I just pray that we have a happy ending, and we get Angela out safe."

"That makes two of us," Mateo said as they both started to walk away.

Teagan remained behind the doorway a moment, absorbing what she'd just heard.

Hudson and Mateo were going to leave tonight to rescue Angela.

And she wasn't supposed to know.

The two of them could be walking into a death trap.

If she knew the Farinos—and she did—they wouldn't think twice about killing Hudson, Mateo, and Sienna.

But they wouldn't kill Teagan.

Not while her baby was still inside her.

Her thoughts raced as she tried to figure out how to keep everyone she cared about safe. She didn't want to make any stupid decisions . . . but she needed to make a choice she could live with.

CHAPTER
THIRTY-SEVEN

TEAGAN WATCHED from her cabana window as Hudson and Mateo loaded the Hummer. She had the lights turned off and was careful to remain in the shadows so no one would see her. The darkness helped.

The men outside moved quietly as they packed as if not wanting to disturb anyone.

Teagan had to figure out a way to help.

But she had no car or means of leaving here. Plus, the gate at the entrance required a code. There was no way she could walk away from this place and expect to find help either.

As soon as Hudson and Mateo went back into the office for more supplies, Teagan hurried toward the Hummer, dark blanket in hand.

Quickly, she darted onto the back seat floor and lay there, covering herself with the blanket.

She didn't know if her plan would work.

But it was worth a shot.

Once the blanket covered her—completely, she hoped—her heart thumped in her ears.

A few minutes later, voices approached and then a door opened. The back hatch slammed shut before Mateo and Hudson climbed inside the front.

A moment of sheer panic hit her.

Sienna. Would she climb into the back seat? They'd said she was helping them.

Teagan held her breath, counting the seconds until the back door opened and she'd be exposed.

But it didn't happen.

Instead, the Hummer started, and they headed down the road.

Sienna must be travelling another way.

Relief spread through her, leaving her shaken.

That was a close call. Too close.

So far, the guys were quiet.

Good.

It didn't feel as intrusive if they didn't talk when she could overhear.

Still, guilt pounded inside her.

She shouldn't be here.

But she'd been desperate.

She hoped she didn't regret this.

* * *

Hudson stared at the dark road in front of him.

They'd gone through the logistics of their plans

several times. Now he only hoped their strategy worked.

"Any updates on the Benjamin Soldier situation?" Mateo asked as they passed time.

"Not that I know. I only know Charlie hired some guy named Ruger to look into that terrorist attack fifteen years ago in Florida."

"You really think someone else was responsible, besides the terrorists?"

Hudson shrugged. "Nothing will surprise me anymore."

Charlie believed there was more to her father's death than the government let on. When she wasn't rescuing women and horses, she was using her time and resources to find out more information about his death.

Unfortunately, four people from her father's squadron were now dead.

The person responsible for their deaths was behind bars, but questions remained.

They arrived back at the familiar airstrip, where Ghost was waiting for them. As Hudson climbed from the Hummer to unload the gear, he thought he saw a movement in the back seat.

He reached for his gun as he watched.

Someone had tossed a blanket inside.

The air left his lungs as a face appeared from beneath it.

"Teagan . . ." Hudson opened the door. "What do you think you're doing?"

She climbed out, a sheepish look on her face. "I had to come."

His gaze continued to darken. "You aren't supposed to know about this."

"Well, I do. And they're going to kill you."

"And they're not going to kill you?"

Her hand covered her belly. "No, actually they won't."

His hands went to his hips as his jaw tightened. "So, you're going to trade yourself for Angela? Is that your plan?"

"It's the only way to save her. They're not going to hurt me while I'm pregnant."

"And after?" Anger tinged his voice.

"Then I'll figure things out."

He stepped closer. "No, you won't. Because as soon as that baby is born, they'll have no reason to keep you alive. And they will be keeping an even better eye on you until then. There won't be a chance for escape. Don't you understand that?"

"I understand the risk I'm taking."

"But what about your baby?"

Tears filled her gaze. "I'm going to get away with my child. I'll figure out a way."

***

Teagan stared at Hudson, waiting for his reaction.

His body appeared wired and ready to explode.

But he wasn't the exploding type.

"Now what am I supposed to do?" He threw his hands up, still in control. "I can't leave you here, and I can't take you with me."

"You *can* take me with you."

"No, I can't—I won't. Do you know why? Because if you come, I'm going to be distracted. And I can't afford to be distracted right now."

"I'll stay out of your way."

"I left you back at the ranch so I wouldn't have to worry about you."

She stepped closer, ready to plead with him. "I can't sit back and do nothing."

"That's exactly what you need to be doing right now. You should've trusted us to handle this. You should've trusted *me*."

She wanted to argue with him, but she knew she couldn't. He was right. She had no business being here.

"What are you going to do?" she asked.

His gaze locked with hers. "That's exactly what I'm going to need to figure out. Let's just hope we don't run out of time in the process."

HUDSON STARED at Teagan as they exited the airplane after landing in Dallas. "Just because we didn't have time to take you back to the ranch, doesn't mean you're going to get Angela with us. You're staying here with Ghost."

Her eyes widened first with shock and then with defiance. "What? No. I need to go with you. I need to help."

"You can help by staying out of the way."

"What about Sienna? I thought you needed her, but she didn't come with us. Maybe I can help instead?"

"Sienna is already here. She's in position. Waiting for us."

Her shoulders drooped. "Hudson . . ."

He stepped closer. "I won't be able to live with myself if something happens to you. Do you understand that? I've already had to bury you once. I don't want to do it again."

She looked away briefly, moisture gathering in her eyes, but he could still see the defiance in her gaze.

Finally, she stepped back and nodded. "Okay. Fine."

Good. She would stay here. Even if she didn't look happy about it.

Still, he'd rather have her unhappy and alive than dead.

He glanced at Ghost. "I need you to keep an eye on her."

He nodded. "Will do."

With one more glance at Teagan, Hudson stepped toward the Hummer waiting for them in the distance. The ranch kept a couple of vehicles at each airport they frequently used. It beat trying to arrange for transportation every time they flew somewhere.

They didn't have any more time to waste.

If they were going to rescue Angela, they needed to go now.

Teagan paced the small airport lobby, unable to sit still.

This private airport was tiny. The lobby had a reception desk. Two locked offices were against one wall. On the opposite wall was a unisex bathroom and a small vending area.

The front wall was all windows so people could see planes coming and going. Two couches and four padded chairs were artfully arranged.

Aside from Teagan and Ghost, the airport was empty.

She had her pick of seats. But Teagan had no desire to sit.

Her nerves were too on edge.

Hudson and Mateo had left thirty minutes ago to meet Sienna.

From what Teagan understood, they should be getting close to the location where the tradeoff was supposed to happen.

Ghost stood near the door, looking out into the darkness as if watching for trouble. The two hadn't said much to each other. Then again, what was there to say?

Teagan felt better off praying and pacing.

And that's exactly what she was doing.

But fifteen minutes later, she couldn't stay quiet anymore.

"Have you heard anything from them?" She paused in front of Ghost.

He shook his head and drew his gaze away from the window. "Not yet."

"They should be there by now."

"They very well could be. They're not giving me a play-by-play of what's going down."

"But what if they need help?"

"Hudson, Mateo, and Sienna are great. Just be patient with them."

"I'm trying to be." Teagan paused, trying to distract herself. "How long have you worked with them?"

He crossed his arms and turned toward her slightly

so he could look between the outside and her. "Not that long, only a few months."

"I hear you were a fighter pilot."

"That's right. When I got out, I worked for a commercial airline for a few years, and I hated it. Now, I pilot private jets. Whenever I can, I help out Charlie and the gang."

"Sounds like an interesting job."

"It is. You should meet some of the clients I've flown. They have more money than they know what to do with. Some of them have more fame than they know what to do with. And more power."

"That fits the description of the Farinos to a T."

"I imagine it does." He glanced at her again. "I can't imagine what it would've been like to live with that family the past two years."

She tightened her arms across her chest. "You don't want to imagine it. I wouldn't wish it on anybody. That's why I need to get my friend Angela away from them."

"Just give it a little more time." His voice dipped with compassion. "This may not happen quickly. But at least you can know you have some of our best guys working on it."

THIRTY-NINE

HUDSON AND MATEO picked up Sienna a couple of miles away from the site where they were supposed to meet the Farinos, and Sienna drove them the rest of the way there.

But when they arrived, there was nothing out there.

Years ago, this had probably been a thriving production plant of some sort.

It looked like it had been abandoned for a long time.

The asphalt was faded with weeds growing in the cracks. There were no overhead lights.

Only darkness.

And a wide-open space without any options for places to hide.

This was the way the Farinos had planned it, no doubt. Brilliant on their part.

Mateo hid in the back of the vehicle beside a small hole in the back door that his gun barrel fit through. It also allowed him to see what was going on.

Hudson lay on the floor in the back seat, while Sienna sat behind the wheel. He had a blanket ready to cover himself, but he didn't need to do so yet.

His heart thumped in his ears as he waited.

He hoped this worked.

They'd bet everything on it.

"See anyone yet?" he asked Sienna.

"Negative."

No one was here.

He glanced at his watch. He still had five minutes until the tradeoff.

And he wasn't sure how this would go down.

Because certainly they just weren't going to hand Angela over. Especially not when they realized that Sienna was not Teagan.

After another minute, he lifted up and scanned everything around him again, remembering that bomb that had been left in that cabin.

Was this simply another setup? Was there some kind of a dangerous surprise waiting for them here?

If they truly thought that Teagan would be here, then probably not. They wouldn't risk hurting her and the baby.

He knew she was right when she said they wouldn't kill her as long as she was pregnant.

Flesh and blood meant everything to these people.

Until someone betrayed them.

Then flesh and blood became just another commodity.

Hudson knew all about this family and how they

operated. Their power and control were no secret, and they'd even made the national news at times for crimes they were being investigated for.

"See anything?" Sienna glanced at him, her wig a surprising match to Teagan's formerly blonde hair.

From a distance, she very well could pass as Teagan. They were approximately the same size, even though Teagan was taller.

He shook his head. "Not yet. I have a bad feeling about this."

"Me too. Just what are they planning exactly?"

"That's what I'm wondering too. And being here right now . . . we're sitting ducks."

Sienna glanced at her watch. "Three minutes. That's how much time we're supposed to have until we meet them. Until then, I guess we have no choice except to sit tight."

***

Anxiety was getting the best of Teagan.

Every second that passed seemed painfully slow.

She and Ghost had chatted a little more. But he mostly remained stationed by the window as if waiting for trouble.

Teagan feared someone knew they were here. She knew Hudson and the gang were smart. Certainly, they hadn't blabbed to anyone listening who they were and where they were.

But the Farinos were also shrewd. Would they have been able to figure out where she was?

She wasn't sure.

She reached into her pocket and pulled out a picture.

The picture of her and Hudson from the day they'd gotten engaged.

The photo she'd taken with her when she'd been forced to flee from her home with the Farinos.

It had been in her pocket when she'd been shopping. She'd brought it with her today also.

She ran her hand over Hudson's image, a bad feeling in her gut.

She didn't want things to end poorly between them.

If she had all the desires of her heart, she'd admit that she wanted things to end with her and Hudson together. With her baby. Forever.

But hoping for that seemed too risky right now.

Just then, a light flickered in the distance, and she glanced up.

Ghost must have seen it too because he straightened. Suddenly, he was entirely on guard.

"Ghost . . ."

He pushed his hand back toward her. "Stay where you are."

"Are those headlights?"

"That's what it looks like. But no one else is supposed to be here tonight."

Teagan held her breath, a bad feeling swirling in her gut.

She watched as the lights got closer and closer.

Maybe it was just someone who worked at the airport. Or a late-night flight that had just been scheduled. Or maybe it was security for this facility.

Even as all the thoughts rushed through her head, she doubted any were true.

How much protection would that glass in front of them offer?

Teagan wasn't sure.

She glanced around, looking for anywhere they might be able to hide or anything that she might be able to use as a weapon.

She saw nothing.

Ghost drew his gun as he stood there.

The headlights stopped in front of the building. From what she could tell through the darkness, it looked like a SUV.

As one of the windows rolled down, she held her breath.

"Go into the bathroom!" Ghost shouted. "And lock the door."

Just as he said the words, bullets sprayed through the front windows.

Glass shattered as the smoky scent of gunpowder filled the air.

Teagan ducked behind the reception desk, covering her head with her hands.

Her heart pounded in her ears.

Was Ghost okay?

"Teagan . . . run!" Ghost said.

They'd been ambushed, she realized.

Somehow Farino and his guys had known they were going to be here, hadn't they?

"Teagan, go. Now!"

Staying low, she headed toward the small bathroom she'd used earlier.

Just as she stepped into the bathroom, a shadow fell over her.

Someone else was in this building.

Teagan had a feeling that the bullets that had just sprayed the front of this facility had all just been a cover for this moment.

THE FARINOS WERE SUPPOSED to meet here with Angela fifteen minutes ago.

Apprehension thrummed inside Hudson.

"Something's wrong," he said.

Sienna nodded. "I agree. But what?"

"We should get back to the airport and make sure everything's okay there. First, let me call Ghost."

Hudson grabbed his phone and dialed his colleague's number.

The device rang several times before going to voicemail.

More tension snaked its way up his spine.

Hudson immediately tried to call him again but had the same results. "Why wouldn't he answer?"

Mateo sat up from where he was laying. "I'd say maybe he's out of range, but I think you and I both know that's not true."

"Keep trying to call him, Sienna," Hudson insisted. "I'll drive us back to the airport."

Sienna moved from the driver's seat, and Hudson took her place then cranked the engine.

Pressing the accelerator, he drove—probably too quickly—away from the parking lot.

He was thirty minutes away from the airport.

A lot could happen in thirty minutes.

Teagan should have never come with him on this mission. He wished he had known. Wished there was some way he could have stopped her.

But it was too late to change that now.

Right now, he just needed to move. Just needed to get back to that airport and see whatever was happening for himself.

Time was running out, and he knew there was no way he could get there quickly enough.

This had all just been a setup, hadn't it?

***

Teagan sat in the back of a sedan. Two gunmen sat on either side of her, while another man drove.

Farino's men, she had no doubt. She didn't recognize them, but she knew.

One had been waiting for her in the back of that building, just counting down the moments until the opportunity presented itself to grab her.

They must have come with two cars, the one in the front that had sprayed the bullets and distracted them.

Then one with the lights out that had gone to the back of the building where one of these guys had snuck inside.

"Where are you taking me?" she asked.

"It's not important," the man beside her said.

"You don't have to do this, you know." It was a desperate plea and one that probably wouldn't work, but she felt like she needed to try anyway.

Things were not supposed to happen like this.

The way it was looking now, the Farinos would have her in their custody and also have Angela.

Nothing would have been resolved.

But since Farino's men were here, maybe Hudson, Mateo, and Sienna were okay.

Maybe they hadn't had to fight anyone.

Hudson . . .

An ache formed in her chest.

She should've stayed at Vanishing Ranch. That was clear.

But it wasn't her nature to sit back and watch while people she loved were hurt.

And the Farinos had known that.

She tried to look out the window, tried to pick up clues on where they might be taking her.

They were too smart to take her back to one of their houses.

Except she knew they probably had properties that weren't listed on any legal documents. That was just the kind of people they were. She wasn't even sure if the cabin they'd blown up had been recorded as theirs.

As the miles stretched outside, she couldn't get the image of Hudson out of her mind.

Or those words that he had told her.

I've already had to bury you once. I don't want to do it again.

Tears pressed at Teagan's eyes.

Everything was backfiring.

He would come looking for her.

She knew he would.

The Farinos knew that also.

They'd have some kind of plan in place.

Instead of keeping the people she loved safe, it appeared she was just putting them in more danger.

CHAPTER
FORTY-ONE

HUDSON SUCKED in a breath when they pulled up to the airport and saw the scene in front of him.

The overhead lights flickered inside. The front windows were shattered, mere shards hanging onto the frame. Bullet holes pierced everything in sight, and casings littered the ground.

"What happened here?" Sienna muttered beside him.

They hadn't been able to get up with Ghost yet.

Any of the possible excuses Hudson had thought about as to why his colleague wasn't answering disappeared.

This was a worst-case scenario.

Hudson threw the SUV into Park and rushed out, his gun drawn.

He didn't see any other vehicles around, but he had to play it safe. Just in case.

Sienna and Mateo remained on his heels as he carefully stepped into the building.

He glanced around, searching for any signs of life.

Had Farino's men shown up here and taken Teagan and Ghost?

If that was the case, then Ghost was a goner.

A lump formed in Hudson's throat at the thought.

He, Mateo, and Sienna split up, each taking a separate side of the building. The facility wasn't large, but they had no time to waste.

As he hurried toward the reception area, he froze. Two feet stuck out from behind the desk.

"Ghost . . ."

Hudson quickly holstered his gun and rushed toward his friend.

His heart beat harder when he saw the blood, bruises, and cuts covering Ghost's face. When he saw the lifeless body.

No . . .

Hudson knelt beside his friend and shook his shoulders. "Ghost?"

When Ghost didn't stir, Hudson put a finger to his neck.

He still had a heartbeat.

Hudson didn't see any major wounds.

Maybe there was still hope . . .

"Ghost . . ." He shook his friend again.

This time, one of his eyes popped open.

Relief filled Hudson.

Maybe Ghost would be okay.

But their problems were far from over.

Sienna appeared beside him. "It's clear."

"Call 911."

"On it." Sienna pulled out her phone.

"Where's Teagan?" Hudson locked gazes with his friend, and he prayed that Ghost could respond.

"They . . . took . . . her . . ."

Hudson didn't have to ask who. He knew.

The Farinos.

Ghost began to ramble. "XM3 . . . 7QV . . . XM3 7QV . . ."

"What are you trying to say?" Hudson wasn't sure if his friend was loopy or not.

Finally, he managed to mutter, "License . . . plate."

Ghost had memorized the license plate of the vehicle Teagan had been taken in.

His breath left him in a whoosh.

Maybe there was hope of finding Teagan.

Hudson stored the plate number in his memory.

He needed to call Brody.

As he grabbed his phone, something on the floor caught his eye.

A photo of him and Teagan.

From the night they'd gotten engaged.

His breath caught.

Had Teagan brought that with her? Had she somehow smuggled it into her belongings when the Farinos grabbed her?

He swallowed down his emotions.

He would fight with everything in him to get her

back—to both make sure she was safe and to win her heart again.

Thirty minutes later, the car Teagan was in pulled to a stop in front of a large estate in the middle of the woods.

No other buildings were located within miles of this place. Teagan had paid attention as they drove.

No doubt, the Farinos had planned to isolate her. To make it so she'd have nowhere to run.

She didn't recognize this place. She hadn't been here before.

But she knew it was theirs.

One of her guards opened the door and stepped out. He grabbed her arm before she could make any moves and yanked her out, squeezing her arm so hard that a small yelp escaped.

The other guard slipped out behind her, blocking her other side.

"You don't have to handle me like that," Teagan said through clenched teeth. She jerked her arm away.

"Apparently, he does." A new voice filled the air.

She knew exactly who it belonged to.

Frank Farino.

She looked up and saw her father-in-law standing there, a glare on his handsome face. "Long time, no see."

"Not long enough," Teagan answered, not willing to cower. "Why did you bring me here?"

"I think you know the answer to that question." His gaze remained distant but possessive.

He was a man who always got what he wanted—and it showed in the way he carried himself.

"You can't force me to stay here against my will."

Her father-in-law stepped closer, looking her up and down before his gaze stopped on her belly. "Oh, I think I can."

Instinctively, Teagan wanted to put her hands over her abdomen. To protect her baby.

But she couldn't.

The two guards flanking her held her arms.

And, right now, she'd never felt so exposed.

Teagan had known the Farinos would keep her alive until her baby was born.

But what would they do to her in the meantime? Lock her in a room? Torture her in just enough ways to cause pain but keep her alive?

She didn't know.

She didn't want to find out.

She swallowed hard as dread filled her.

But she wouldn't let him see her fear.

Instead, Teagan shot daggers with her eyes. "What did you do with Angela?"

"Does it really matter? I think you have bigger worries right now."

FORTY-TWO

"I NEED you to track down the car associated with this license plate number and see if it has a built-in GPS. Then I need to know where it went."

Hudson paced the airport lobby, talking on the phone with Brody.

The man was brilliant. If anyone could figure this out, it was him.

Paramedics had arrived on the scene and were checking out Ghost. Mateo and Sienna were giving their statements to the police.

The FBI was on the way.

There was no reason to keep the feds from this anymore. Not now that the Farinos had Teagan. All their promises were out the window.

But Hudson didn't have time to wait for the agency to get here.

Every second counted.

"This is going to take some time," Brody muttered. "I'm going to have to hack into some systems . . ."

"We don't have a lot of time." Hudson paused near the broken window, his jaw tightening.

"The pressure isn't helping . . ."

"Sorry. But people's lives are on the line."

"I'm aware."

Hudson heard keys tapping in the background, and knew his friend was doing his best.

He'd apologize for his impatience later.

At the moment, all he could think about was finding Teagan.

If she slipped away now, he might not ever find her again. The Farinos would tuck her away somewhere no one would ever suspect.

He knew how these things worked. As many connections as this family had, they also had all the resources in the world at their disposal. They could whisk Teagan away to an island where she'd never be seen again.

Hudson couldn't let that happen.

Not that Hudson would stop trying to find her.

Because even after everything that had happened between them, he still loved Teagan. He knew that without a doubt.

A new surge of protectiveness rose inside him.

The baby growing inside Teagan wasn't his. But it didn't matter. The baby was a part of her now. Hudson would do whatever was needed to keep the child safe.

But first, he had to find Teagan.

More tension snaked up his spine as Hudson pressed the phone to his ear. "Anything?"

"Actually . . ." Brody's voice lilted upward. "I think I might have found something that can help you. Just give me a second to confirm I'm correct. I think we can both agree that mistakes aren't an option right now."

The guards had taken Teagan inside the house, a place where no expense had been spared, from the natural stone flooring beneath her, the exotic hardwood beams above, and the designer-selected decor.

Of course. Teagan hadn't expected anything else from the self-important Farinos.

The guards forced her to sit in a chair, and Frank stood in front of her.

An evil look seemed to saturate his gaze.

Frank . . . with his classic Italian looks and slight accent. He had olive skin, surprisingly dark hair, and a thick mustache that he seemed to take pride in. He wasn't thin or fat—somewhere in between, and he favored wearing designer suits that cost more than some people made in a month.

The two guards remained close, and Teagan saw another armed guard lingering in the doorway. Those were just the thugs she could see.

She had no doubt that there were more lurking around here.

"Where's Angela?" She glared at Frank as she asked the question.

"She's alive . . . for now. I've always known you've had a soft spot for people you care about. That's why I know you'll do anything for the baby growing inside you."

Teagan sucked in a breath, and her head began to spin.

Even though she'd realized the Farinos knew about her pregnancy, hearing the words leave Frank's lips made ice-cold fear shoot through her.

"You didn't think you were going to be able to keep this little secret, now, did you?" He raised his eyebrows in a smirk, as if he'd enjoyed her reaction.

She continued to glare at him. "How did you find out?"

She'd wondered that from the start. She'd been so careful. It just didn't seem possible that they'd discovered her secret.

"We have our ways," he muttered.

"But I didn't tell anyone." Had it been Art? Had he somehow found out?

Frank glanced in the distance and nodded at someone.

A moment later, Angela emerged from a doorway.

All the breath left Teagan's lungs as she stared at her friend.

Her uninjured friend.

Her unbound friend who freely walked toward her wearing clean, expensive clothes and fresh makeup.

Even her dark hair with its honey highlights looked salon-styled.

A Maltese pranced along beside her.

She looked nothing like a woman in captivity.

Teagan reeled, feeling as if she'd been punched in the gut. "What happened to all the bruises and the blood from the video?"

"I'm sorry." Angela stopped in front of her, her expression still stoic.

She didn't even act like the same person Teagan had worked with at the animal rescue—the woman who was down-to-earth and caring and not afraid to get dirty.

Had they drugged her? Brainwashed her?

Or had Teagan simply been blind to who she was the whole time?

Either way, this new Angela left Teagan feeling off-balance.

"They came to me and offered to pay me a pretty penny to keep an eye on you," Angela said.

"Angela . . ." The word came out just above a whisper.

The one person Teagan had thought was her friend really wasn't.

Angela had been bought and paid for, Teagan realized.

Bile churned inside Teagan at the thought.

"I didn't mean for any of it to happen this way." Angela shrugged, her gaze nearly emotionless. "They didn't leave me much choice."

"It doesn't look like you're here against your own free will." The words came out through gritted teeth.

Angela shrugged again. "I guess I'm a lot like you. I did what I had to do to survive. Besides, being here isn't that bad."

Her statement nearly felt like a slap in the face.

"Is that so? You have no idea."

Teagan had been forced into this life. She'd been unable to get away.

From the looks of it, that wasn't the case with Angela.

But she wouldn't put anything past Frank Farino. To him, anyone and everyone was expendable.

Anger simmered inside Teagan. "Whatever they paid you, I hope it was worth it. I can't believe you'd do this to me . . ."

"I've worked so hard my entire life, yet I could barely pay the rent on my dingy apartment. There was no hope of me getting ahead. Then I had some medical testing done about a year ago. Thankfully, nothing turned up. But those bills left me in even more debt. That's when the Farinos came to me and offered to help."

Realization tightened Teagan's lungs. "When was that?"

"Six months ago," she answered. "It's the only reason I agreed to let you volunteer. They gave me some extra 'donations' to help make ends meet. The deal seemed simple enough at first."

"And then?" Teagan tried not to scowl, but how could she not?

Angela was talking so nonchalantly about this.

Meanwhile, Teagan had risked everything to help Angela . . . someone she'd considered a friend.

"Then they asked me to do other things. To monitor what you were doing. To plant something on my computer in case you ever used it. I didn't think much of their requests. I didn't think I was hurting anyone."

Teagan only stared at Angela and shook her head in disbelief—and disgust.

"Then I found the pregnancy test in the bathroom trash can." Angela shrugged. "I knew you had left it there. I reviewed the security footage of everyone who'd come into the facility that day. The only ones who'd used that restroom were you, me, and three men."

"So, you sold me out?"

The first sincere look of regret filled her gaze. "I knew that discovery was my magic bullet. The Farinos gave me an even bigger payout for that news. I was going to be able to move into a better apartment. Maybe, I could finally get ahead."

"So, you sold your soul for some cash." Teagan shook her head. "I thought more of you. You really acted like you loved those animals. You should win an award for that."

Angela's eyes softened for the first time. "I also want to use some of the money for the shelter. I really do love the animals there . . ."

Teagan stared at her, not believing a word she said.

Angela lowered her gaze, just for a moment appearing as if she were ashamed. "I never thought all of this would happen. If you hadn't disappeared . . ."

"Then you would have been able to keep spying on me? Instead, they got you to lure me out."

Angela said nothing.

What was there to say?

"Enough of this talk! It's exhausting me." Frank kneeled in front of Teagan, his eyes still on her belly as if that was all that mattered, as if he hadn't heard the conversation that had just transpired. "Is it a boy or a girl?"

Bile rose in Teagan's throat, and she raised her chin. "I don't know yet."

"I think you do." His voice deepened in a subtle threat before he repeated, "Is it a boy or a girl?"

Teagan's heart thrummed harder at his demanding tone.

"I don't know." Her words came out harder, almost biting.

Frank narrowed his eyes, a new coolness washing over him. "We'll find out soon enough. My Lucia is very excited about becoming a grandmother, as you can imagine. Of course, she doesn't want to be called Grandma. That will make my beautiful wife seem too old. She's thinking about Mimi. What are your thoughts on that?"

Teagan scowled at the very idea. If she had anything

to do with it, her child would never meet Frank and Lucia.

But it wouldn't benefit her to say that now.

"If that's what Lucia likes," she said instead.

"She does. And I would hate for anyone to make her unhappy. Just as I hated to see my son suffer. I'll do whatever I can to protect those I love." He twisted his head slightly as he observed her. "I guess you understand that."

"I do," Teagan said through gritted teeth.

"Can you imagine someone taking a brand-new grandbaby away from the grandparents? That would be heartless, wouldn't it?"

Teagan knew she couldn't argue, that if she did it would only harm her in the long run.

But it pained her to agree.

Still, she forced herself to say, "It would."

"So, are we having a grandson or a granddaughter?" he repeated.

"I don't know yet."

"I think you do." His gaze darkened. "Tell me."

He glanced across the room, giving some type of silent signal.

Teagan braced herself for whatever would happen next.

One of Frank's guards grabbed Angela and shoved a gun to her head.

Her friend—or former friend—gasped.

Teagan didn't think her fear was an act this time.

Angela had honestly thought she was protected, that she was safe now that she was in the Farinos' pockets.

Little did she know . . .

"Tell me or we'll shoot her," Frank growled.

Teagan's gaze lingered on Angela. Even though her friend had betrayed her, she didn't want to see it end like this.

The terror on Angela's face looked real.

Her backstabbing friend had no idea what she'd gotten herself into.

Teagan glanced back at Frank. There was no use in delaying the news.

She hadn't told anyone yet that Dr. Cossette had done an ultrasound.

She knew the sex of her baby.

"A boy." Her teeth remained clenched as she said the words. "Are you happy now?"

A grin stretched across Frank's face. "A boy? He'll be Little Ricky."

Little Ricky?

No way.

The thought made her want to throw up.

Without invitation, Frank reached forward and placed his hand on Teagan's belly.

She tried to revolt, to pull away, but she couldn't.

There was nowhere for her to go.

"I'll set you up with another ultrasound so we can make sure the baby's doing okay," Frank said. "You won't leave our side. We'll bring in a nutritionist to plan your meals. We'll provide the best prenatal care money can buy. I have to know that my grandson is safe . . . because he's the only thing that's important to me."

Teagan heard the underlying truth in his words.

She was nothing.

Just an incubator.

And she had no doubt that her father-in-law would kill her as soon as his grandson was born.

HUDSON STAYED on the line with Brody as he and Mateo jumped in the car. Sienna stayed behind with Ghost, to make sure he was all right and to be a liaison with the FBI.

"How far away does it say we are?" Mateo asked as he cranked the engine.

"About an hour." Hudson's fists clenched as he said the words.

A lot could happen in an hour.

As if Mateo could read his mind, he pressed the accelerator harder as they sped away from the airport.

"When was the last time they moved?" Hudson asked Brody, his phone on speaker so Mateo could hear and so he could keep an eye on the map Brody had sent.

"Let's see . . . they've been in this location at least thirty minutes. It looks like this is where they stopped."

"Can you look up any information you can find on the address?"

"On it."

Hudson heard the keys tapping again.

The darkened landscape flew by around them—but not nearly fast enough for his tastes right now.

He kept an eye on the screen so he could instruct Mateo on where to go.

"Okay, I think I've got something," Brody said. "It looks like the address where they stopped is 1020 Broadmoor Lane. It's a pretty large estate outside of Dallas."

"Who owns it?" Hudson asked.

"It's registered to Gilcrest Enterprises."

"And who owns Gilcrest Enterprises?" Hudson didn't mean to snap, but he knew he had.

"I'm looking . . . it appears someone named Sylvia Preston." More keys tapped. "And Sylvia Preston is actually the maiden name of Sylvia Farino . . . Ron Farino's wife."

Anger burned inside Hudson.

These people were so twisted.

The Farinos had definitely grabbed Teagan.

The whole family was in on it.

What he wasn't sure about was what exactly they were doing with her now.

The more time that passed, the less likely it would be they could get her back. That meant that one wrong move could end in catastrophe.

That wasn't an option right now.

Hudson needed to let the FBI know more details about what was going on.

Because if he knew the Farinos like he thought he did, there was no way he and Mateo were getting on this estate just the two of them.

They'd need a whole team in order to rescue Teagan.

And they didn't have much time to coordinate it.

Teagan had been left alone in the large room.

Her hands were tied behind her, and her legs had been secured to a wooden chair placed in the center of the space.

Frank had said something about going to get Lucia.

When he'd left, he'd escorted Angela away with him.

Teagan's former friend had cast one last look over her shoulder as she left the room with her little dog. Angela looked shaken but otherwise unharmed.

At the moment.

She still didn't fully grasp the danger she was in, did she?

Angela's betrayal stung.

Then again, maybe Teagan should have known better than to trust Angela. She knew the Farinos. Knew how they operated. She should have assumed they would plant someone at that shelter.

But in a moment of optimism, she had let hope take over.

What was she going to do now?

From what she'd observed on the way here, there was nothing around this house except miles and miles of private land.

Was it even a possibility that Hudson could find her?

She didn't think so.

How would he? She didn't have a phone or anything else to track her location with.

Despair tried to press into her.

She held back.

As long as I'm still alive, there is still hope.

That's what she'd told herself when she'd almost given up before. She needed to cling to that sentiment now as well.

But as she glanced around, she didn't see anything that could help her—no potential weapons or objects she could use to break free from the ropes binding her wrists and ankles.

If she couldn't find a physical object to use, then she needed instead to look for the right opportunity.

Just as the thought went through her head, an interior door leading into the room rattled.

Tension twisted inside her.

Who was coming now?

And what were they planning on doing?

FORTY-FOUR

"PULL over right here and cut the headlights." Hudson checked the map on his screen and pointed to the side of the road.

Mateo did as he asked.

They stashed the car behind some trees. They would go the rest of the way on foot.

Hudson didn't waste any time climbing from the car and quietly closing the door.

Teagan was close—yet she felt so far at the same time.

He and Mateo started forward, stealthily moving through the dark woods. They paused when they reached a fence that surrounded the house.

Two flashlights shone in the distance.

Guards were patrolling.

The Farinos weren't taking any chances. This place was going to be like Fort Knox.

"What's our plan?" Mateo stared at the property in the distance.

Hudson glanced around. "I know we have backup on the way. Last I heard, they're still thirty minutes away, however. I'm afraid we don't have that much time."

"So, you want to go in?"

His jaw tightened. "I want to get closer to assess the situation. Then we're going to have to be very careful."

"We can do this."

They stayed along the edge of the fence as they crept closer to the sprawling house.

They were too far away to see much. But Hudson noted where the lights were on inside.

That was where they needed to go.

He hoped this hadn't been a wild goose chase. He prayed this truly was where Teagan had been taken.

But these guys were smart. He wouldn't put it past them to switch vehicles to throw them off their tail.

Just then, a scream cut through the air.

A woman's scream.

Teagan?

His heart rate ratcheted.

He had to find out.

"We don't have any time to waste," Hudson muttered. "Let's go."

As they started toward the house, a figure stepped out from behind a tree.

One of the guards.

Based on the smirk on his face, this guy was looking forward to whatever was about to happen next.

Hudson vowed one thing—this guy was going to regret standing in the way of him and Teagan.

Teagan's lungs froze when she heard the scream.

Was that . . . Angela?

Her heart pounded harder.

What was happening in the other room?

A moment later, Frank stepped back inside. He held a knife in his hands—a large one. He wiped the blade with a cloth, carefully examining it.

A knife?

Was there blood on it?

She couldn't be sure.

Teagan tried to draw herself back.

What was Frank thinking right now? Certainly, he knew that the baby was too young to survive outside of her womb, right?

Teagan didn't know, but she didn't like all the scenarios going through her head.

"I'm back," he announced. "I had to take care of some business."

Angela's face rushed through her mind.

Had he done something to her? Had he used her for their purposes and then disposed of her?

Teagan wouldn't put it past Frank—or anyone in the family, for that matter.

Despite what happened between her and Angela, she didn't like the idea of her being harmed.

"What have you done?" Her voice cracked as she asked the question.

Frank shrugged. "Maybe you'll find out . . . eventually. It's not important now."

"Why is violence always the answer for you?" Teagan asked.

Frank glanced up as if that question had surprised him. "Violence? What are you talking about? I tried reasoning first."

"Did you?" She'd seen the way he interacted with people. He didn't reason with people. He manipulated them.

Teagan couldn't understand how it was that someone became this obsessed with money and power.

But that's the way it was with this family.

They could never have enough of either of those things. The more they got, the more they wanted.

And Ricky had been their only chance of producing an heir to the empire they'd created through crime, coercion, and other illegal means.

When he died, all of their dreams had crashed.

Teagan had seen the panic in their eyes along with the grief. Because they truly had grieved for him.

But before the grief could subside, vengeance had kicked in.

"You were the perfect woman for our son." Frank paused in front of her again. "Lucia and I agreed."

"Your wife hated me from the start."

"She's just hard to please. Don't let that get to you." He flashed a smile as if he knew exactly what she was talking about.

"What are you going to do with me?" Teagan cut to the chase.

"We have a wonderful room set up for you. Not here in Dallas. That would be too easy."

She froze. She didn't like the sound of that. "Where is it?"

"Does it really matter?" He stepped closer and chuckled again.

She lifted her chin, unwilling to show defeat. "It does matter. It matters to the people who care about me. It matters to *me*."

"You do realize that Teagan Murphy no longer exists on paper, right? It's a little hard to file a missing person's report on someone who doesn't exist."

"There are people who know I'm alive. People that won't stop looking for me."

A sparkle filled his eyes. "But are there?"

Fear spread through her.

What did he mean by that?

And the even bigger question—did Teagan really want to know?

HUDSON SWUNG his fist and caught the man in his jaw.

With that blow, the guard toppled to the ground unconscious.

Mateo rushed toward him and paused when he saw the man lying there. "Good job."

"Thanks." Hudson tucked the man's gun into his waistband. "What about the other guy?"

Another man had come in behind them, thinking he would sneak up on them.

It didn't work.

"I put him in a headlock until he passed out. We should be good for now."

"Perfect. Because I heard a scream, and I need to know what's going on in there."

"Let's go."

They raced toward the house. Headed toward the lit window.

As they got closer, voices drifted from inside.

Hudson ducked low beneath the window to hear.

Teagan.

One of those voices belonged to Teagan.

Carefully, he peered into the room.

She was in the living room. Tied to a chair.

Frank Farino stood in front of her, a knife in his hands.

A knife? Certainly, he wasn't going to use that on Teagan. Or had he already?

He didn't know. But she was still alive. And he didn't see any blood on her.

However . . .

What exactly was Frank planning?

As the thoughts raced through Hudson's head, the conversation floated out to him.

"Believe me when I tell you that we *will* kill him this time," Frank said.

"No, please don't." Teagan's voice trembled. "Hudson didn't do anything. He's nothing like you. He's a good man."

Frank stepped closer. "And I'm not? Is that what you're saying?"

"Depends on how you define a good man. Is it someone who looks after others' well-being or is it someone who attends only to his own interests?"

In some circumstances, Hudson might give Teagan a pat on the back for her brave, honest answer. But not now. Not when her life was on the line.

The next instant, Frank reached forward, and his fingers gripped Teagan's throat.

Hudson bristled, ready to burst through the window to rescue her.

But Mateo stopped him with a hand on his shoulder.

"If it wasn't for my grandbaby growing inside you . . ." Frank growled.

So, they weren't going to kill her.

Not right now, at least.

But Hudson also knew that he couldn't let Teagan out of his sight or, eventually, this wouldn't have a happy ending.

Teagan felt the situation spiraling out of control and knew she needed to do something. To redirect some of Frank's anger.

"Who killed Ricky?" she blurted.

The question seemed to surprise him as his eyes widened. "You know who killed him. The McDonnells. We sent them a message to let them know that they weren't going to get away with it."

"But does that really make sense? I mean, how did they even get into our house?" She'd asked herself that question ever since it happened. She'd sensed there was more to the story, more going on behind the scenes.

"It doesn't matter how they got in," Frank snapped. "All that matters is that we took care of them. An eye for an eye."

Teagan watched as Frank began to pace, knife still in hand.

"But you guys had so much control over the residence," she continued. "You had security systems. Guards. Nobody could get in. All that so I couldn't leave without you guys knowing. Someone had to see something."

"You are making my patience grow thin."

"Do you think that someone outside the family actually got past all those systems you had in place?"

Frank said nothing, he just seemed to listen a moment.

"Besides, why would the McDonnells want to kill him?" She knew her words were a gamble, but it was the only trick she had up her sleeve. "What would they have to gain?"

"Because they knew that killing him would break my heart." He pounded his free hand against his chest.

"Certainly, they had to know that the true way to break your heart would be by getting your money."

"You don't know what you're talking about." His voice turned to a growl.

"Who had the biggest motive to get Ricky out of the way? Someone who wants to inherit your money, that's who."

Frank's gaze darkened. "What are you getting at?"

Teagan knew she'd gotten through to him, that she'd gotten into his head space.

"Think about it—you know the answer already.

Don't you?" She hadn't even realized it herself. Not until now.

But suddenly, everything made sense.

Just as Teagan said the words, a new figure stepped into the room.

Ron Farino.

And Teagan could see the horror of everything clicking into place in Frank's mind.

CHAPTER
FORTY-SIX

HUDSON HELD his breath as he listened to the interchange.

Teagan was on point.

It made perfect sense.

But he wasn't sure if her reveal was going to pay off or if it would backfire.

He remained where he was, watching everything with bated breath, his body poised to act.

Frank and Ron stared at each other a moment.

"She doesn't know what she's talking about," Ron said. "Why would I kill my own nephew?"

"Because you want to take control of this empire when I die," Frank said.

"Then why not just kill you?"

"Because Ricky was next in line. And after Ricky, then my grandbaby." Frank stepped closer, still gripping that knife. "Did you kill my son?"

"I wouldn't do that." Ron's voice sounded eerily calm.

"I think you would. She's right. You're the only person who makes sense. Why didn't I see this earlier?"

"You've got this all wrong—" Ron started.

But the next instant, Ron pulled a gun from his waistband.

He pointed it at his brother's chest.

Around them, the guards stepped into place, each drawing their weapons.

It was a standoff, Hudson realized.

And Teagan was right in the middle of the crossfire.

Teagan couldn't get a deep breath. It didn't matter how hard she tried.

What had she done?

She'd thought that pitting the two brothers against each other might help save her.

But now it was clear that wasn't the case.

The only good news in the situation was that no one's attention was on her at the moment.

She used that opportunity to begin to work the ropes loose around her wrists.

She tried to angle her wrists apart when they'd tied her up.

So she had a little wiggle room.

If she could get these off—along with the ones at her feet—then maybe at the first opportunity she could run.

She didn't know how far she would get.

But at least it was something.

She continued to squirm, trying to wiggle her wrists out of the ropes.

Finally, her binds loosened.

She'd done it.

Her heart beat harder.

A few more tugs, and she'd be free.

But she had to be very careful not to let anyone see.

She glanced at Ron and Frank as they continued to stare down each other.

She'd instigated a war, hadn't she?

Ron with his gun.

Frank with his knife.

And three armed guards surrounding them.

She expected to see all the guns on Ron.

But only two were.

Felix had his gun set on Frank.

He'd been working for Ron this whole time, hadn't he?

That explained why he'd shot at Teagan as she fled the shopping mall with Hudson.

Because, as far as Ron was concerned, she was better off dead too—especially since her baby was the rightful heir to this criminal empire.

Sweat beaded across Teagan's forehead.

How was she going to get out of this?

She should have stayed at Vanishing Ranch. Instead, she had to be headstrong and think she could help.

She pressed her eyes shut a moment as Hudson's face filled her mind.

He might have to sit through another funeral for her.

And she hated herself for putting him in that position.

But as the standoff around her only became more urgent, she didn't see any way she would get out of this situation alive.

"ANY MINUTE NOW, someone's going to pull the trigger and take the first shot," Mateo said.

"I know. There's only one thing I know to do."

"What's that?"

Hudson reached into his backpack and pulled out a smoke bomb. "We throw this through the window. It's going to cause pandemonium. But it might give us just enough time to get in there and grab Teagan and get out before they realize what's happening."

"It's going to be risky. We're outnumbered."

"The FBI is closing in. But we can't wait. I understand if you're not in this with me, though."

"If you're going in, I'm going in," Mateo said.

Some of the tension left his chest, but only for a moment. "Thank you."

With a nod to each other, they knew what to do.

They wouldn't have much time.

Mateo would need to fire his gun through the

window to shatter the glass. Then Hudson would throw the smoke bomb inside, and they would breach the building.

They'd have about sixty seconds to grab Teagan. Escape out the same window. Get back to the car before the smoke dissipated.

Hopefully by that time, the FBI would arrive.

Hudson prayed that was the way everything worked out.

Because one wrong move, and Teagan would be dead.

Teagan felt the rope slip from her wrist. She held the binds in her hands, not willing to risk dropping them to the floor and drawing any attention.

The ropes around her ankles were tighter. Now that her hands were free, she should be able to work the knots.

But how would she do that without being detected?

She wasn't sure.

"You did this, didn't you?" Frank seethed. "You killed my son."

"He would have turned our empire upside down and destroyed it! You and I both know that. Don't be stupid."

"He was . . . my son!" The knife trembled in his hands as he stepped closer. "How could you?"

In a deft move, Ron sidestepped Frank and slipped

behind Teagan, using her as a shield. "Stay back. I'll kill your grandson too. You know I will."

He pulled Teagan closer until she let out a cry.

The guards moved in, ready to take action.

Ron pointed the gun at Teagan. "Call off your men."

"Stand down." Frank didn't hesitate. He held up a hand.

Two of them did. Felix kept his gun out and ready to use.

"I don't know how you can call yourself a Farino." Frank seethed.

The next instant, glass shattered.

Men shouted.

Guns fired.

And then smoke filled the air.

Overwhelming smoke that took her breath away.

Smoke that didn't allow her to see anything that was going on.

Who had done this?

One of Ron's guys?

She didn't know.

She only knew she needed to get down.

In one quick motion, she threw herself to the floor.

The chair cracked.

Quickly, she swung her legs against the floor again. The chair legs completely fell apart.

She pulled her legs out from the ropes.

She was free.

She coughed as smoke filled her lungs.

She just had to make it a little longer. Just had to get away from the smoke.

She began to crawl toward what she thought was the door.

But before she reached it, a hand grabbed her hair. She screamed as someone's strong grip pulled her back to her feet. She felt the hair being pulled from her scalp.

She glanced back.

It was Ron.

And he had a gun to her head.

Teagan knew he wouldn't be afraid to pull that trigger.

FORTY-EIGHT

HUDSON WAVED AWAY the smoke in front of his face.

He was inside.

One obstacle down. Many more to go.

He remained low as he crept forward.

He didn't think that anyone had seen them but, clearly, they knew someone was here. They had to know the smoke bomb had come from somewhere outside.

But the mad scramble of people in this room would work to his advantage.

Or so he thought.

As Hudson looked up, searching for Teagan, he finally spotted her through the haze.

Ron had grabbed her, had his gun to her head.

Hudson's heart dropped into his stomach at the sight of her.

No . . .

But the man's sights seemed to be on someone else.

Hudson knew who he was looking at, even if he couldn't see the man at the moment.

Frank.

Frank grabbed something from his ankle.

A gun.

In one swift motion, the man lifted the weapon in the air.

Aimed it at Ron.

Sneered.

Hudson's breath caught. One miscalculation, and Teagan would be hit.

Then a guttural, "No!" filled the air as he dove forward.

Teagan saw everything happening as if in slow motion.

She saw Frank reach for something.

She felt the barrel of Ron's gun press harder into her temple.

This was it.

The moment she would die.

Then Hudson appeared from the smoke.

Her breath caught.

But she didn't have time to celebrate.

This was far from over.

Ron spotted Hudson also.

He hesitated.

His grip loosened.

When it did, Teagan ducked to the floor.

A bullet exploded through the air.

Then another. And another.

A scream cut through the chaos.

Had that come from her own lips?

She wasn't sure.

When Teagan looked at the floor, she saw the blood there.

Saw the blood on her hands.

Her head swirled.

Had she been hit?

HUDSON HEARD bullets flying through the air.

Heard Teagan scream.

Felt panic.

As Mateo covered him, taking out the other guards, Hudson rushed toward Teagan.

She was on the floor.

Blood surrounded her, covering her hands and pooling at her knees.

No!

He sank down beside her, fearing he'd lose her yet again.

Everything blurred around him.

Nothing else mattered anymore.

Nothing but Teagan.

"Teagan . . ." He touched her face as their eyes met.

"I'm . . . okay."

He quickly scanned her, looking for any signs of where the bullet had hit.

But he saw nothing.

His gaze drifted behind her.

That's when he saw Ron lying on the floor.

Blood gushed from his head and poured all over the floor . . . all over Teagan.

Ron had been hit, not Teagan.

Hudson pulled her into his arms, protecting her from whatever might happen next.

But as the smoke dissipated the house grew quiet.

Mateo stood near the three guards he'd taken down, making sure they didn't awaken and cause any more trouble. One had been shot in the shoulder. Another held his head, and the third was passed out on the floor.

He saw Frank next.

He also lay on the floor, bleeding.

Hudson's heart pounded in his ears.

The two brothers had shot each other, hadn't they?

Just as the question filled his mind, new voices entered the room.

"FBI! Put your hands up!"

Backup . . . they were here.

Maybe this was finally all over.

Teagan pulled the blanket more tightly around her as she sat in the back of the ambulance.

She'd been checked out and, so far, everything looked good. But just to be certain, paramedics had hooked up monitors so they could keep an eye on her.

From where she sat, she'd had a front row seat to see Lucia Farino try to run to her car and escape. Seeing the woman looking so spooked had brought Teagan a brief moment of satisfaction.

But not as much satisfaction as when the FBI had tackled Lucia before reading her rights to her.

The woman deserved to have the book thrown at her.

Right now, Teagan sipped on some water and waited for medics to clear her.

It was dark outside, and flashing lights strobed across the land in front of her.

Hudson lingered there also.

He hadn't let her out of his sight. Even as the FBI interrogated him, he was certain to stand near the ambulance—just in case.

Her heart filled with love at that realization. At the thought that someone was out there who cared about her enough to risk his life to save her.

Love like that didn't come along very often.

Even though Teagan knew he was partly protecting her because it was his job, one look in his eyes and she knew there was more to it than that.

As soon as the FBI agent finished questioning him, Hudson asked the paramedic if he could have a moment.

The paramedic nodded before exiting the ambulance —but still lingering close to monitor her.

Hudson climbed in and took a seat beside her. His

hand gripped hers as he stared into her eyes. "I thought for sure I'd lost you again."

More tears rushed to her eyes. She might as well get used to them . . . at least for the remainder of her pregnancy. "I know. I never should have come."

"Maybe not. But because of what happened tonight, two very dangerous men are off the streets. I wouldn't choose for things to work out the way they did and for you to be in danger, but at least we have a happy ending."

Her eyes met his. "I'm so sorry for everything I put you through."

He squeezed her hand harder. "You don't have to apologize." His voice sounded hoarse as he said the words. "You went through the unimaginable."

Teagan stared at him another moment, unsure what to say.

She knew that she could express her love for Hudson all she wanted. But if he didn't want to be with her and her baby, then none of that mattered.

His lips moved a moment before his mouth closed, almost as if he were trying to find the right words.

Before he could, the paramedic stepped aboard again, something in his hands. "Someone brought us a fetal heart monitor," he explained. "We just want to take every precaution."

"Do you want me to leave?" Hudson asked.

"No, I'd love it if you'd stay."

He continued gripping her hand as the medic put

some gel on a wand before pressing it into her belly. He poked around several seconds before pausing.

A loud pulse sounded through a speaker beside him.

"There it is. A strong, healthy heartbeat."

Relief rushed through her. "It's a beautiful sound."

"Yes, it is." The medic kept the wand in place another moment.

She glanced at Hudson. His eyes were latched onto hers, and he looked enthralled.

"That's . . . amazing," he finally muttered.

Teagan grinned. "Yeah, it is, isn't it?"

The medic put the equipment away and wiped away the extra gel with a tissue. Then he left the ambulance again.

As soon as he was gone, Hudson turned to her. "I love you, Teagan. I always have. I always will. And if you'll let me, I'd be honored to be a part of your baby's life, to make him my own."

Teagan's lungs froze as she comprehended what he had just said. She almost wanted to ask him if he meant it, but she knew he wouldn't have said anything unless he did.

"I would like that very much."

A grin spread across his face.

The next instant, he leaned toward her.

Their lips met.

Despite the storm they'd just gone through, everything in her world felt perfect at that moment.

EPILOGUE

ONE MONTH LATER

AS A KNOCK SOUNDED at Teagan's door, she hurried across the room to answer.

A smile lit her face when she opened it and saw Hudson standing there. He looked handsome in his chambray shirt, jeans, and cowboy hat.

"How are you, gorgeous?" He stepped closer and wrapped his arms around her waist before planting a kiss on her lips.

"I'm better now." Warmth oozed inside her at his touch.

The past month had been wonderful.

Teagan had officially taken a position here at the ranch doing administrative work for them.

That meant she got to see Hudson every day—a fact that delighted her.

She loved the job, loved the area, and loved her newfound freedom.

Every day, she counted her blessings.

"How's the baby?" Hudson murmured as he placed his hand on her stomach.

"He's been busy, moving around a lot."

"Has he?" Hudson's eyebrows shot up. "He's going to be an active little one, huh?"

Teagan grinned. "I think so."

As soon as she said the words, she paused and sucked in a quick breath.

"What is it?" The delight in Hudson's gaze quickly turned to concern.

Teagan took his hand and moved it to the other side of her belly. "Can you feel that?"

"Is that . . . ?" A knot formed between his eyes. Then a smile burst across his face. "Is that . . . the baby kicking?"

"It sure is."

He kissed the top of her head. "That's a beautiful feeling."

"Isn't it?"

"You're going to be a great mom. You know that?"

"I have my doubts at times."

He cupped her face with his hands. "I don't have any."

A sigh of contentment escaped from her.

Angela had survived a knife wound to her chest. She was also awaiting trial for extortion.

Ron Farino died at the scene. Frank had survived and was now behind bars, along with several other members of the Farino family and their employees. Everyone expected him to spend the rest of his life in prison for everything he'd done.

More arrests were coming.

The empire had fallen since the head of the snake had been cut off.

And Teagan was finally safe.

She felt at home here at the ranch, hidden away from the world . . . with Hudson.

He stepped back and reached out his hand. "You ready to go?"

She offered a curtsy as she took his hand. "I am."

The sun was setting outside, and the blue and purple Arizona desert sky was perfect.

Perfect for a wedding.

But it wasn't her and Hudson's wedding.

No, Jesse and Sienna were getting married . . . even though Teagan had originally thought they were already married.

Hudson had filled her in, and it really *was* a long story.

Teagan was honored to be here to share their special day with them.

She stepped outside with Hudson and saw the chairs set up in the pasture. Saw the cross on the stage. Saw the sun setting behind it all.

For a moment, she paused.

What would it be like if she and Hudson were to ever get married?

This would be the perfect location.

She could even imagine her son running around this ranch, burning off energy and petting the horses.

Movement near the mess hall caught her eye.

She stopped on the walkway and squinted.

What was that?

It was a . . . dog?

"Is that . . . ?" She could barely finish her sentence.

It was.

It was Daisy.

Teagan scooted down on the ground as the dog ran into her arms.

She held the animal close, soaking in the scent of the canine and the softness of her fur.

Her heart in her throat, she glanced up at Hudson.

He grinned. "I know you talked about how much this dog meant to you. It took a while, but I was able to adopt her. Sorry it took so long."

"No apologies necessary . . . this is wonderful, Hudson."

His smile widened. "I hoped you'd be happy."

She stood, her gaze latching with his. "You remember when we flew over the Grand Canyon?"

He squinted as if he wasn't sure where she was going with this. "I do."

"You remember how you said that when you stand next to it, you can't take in its greatness. But when you're in the air, far away, suddenly you understand just how vast it is."

"I vaguely remember saying something like that."

"That's how life can be sometimes too, can't it? When we're in the middle of things, often nothing makes sense. But once you get some perspective, everything changes."

Hudson stepped closer. "Is that what this moment is? Perspective?"

She nodded. "Definitely. I would have never imagined a few months ago that I'd be here now. I've had to walk through fire to get to this point—we both have. But looking back . . . I can't complain. Because everything led me to this moment. With you. And Daisy." She rubbed her belly. "And our baby."

Yes, our baby.

She and Hudson had already talked about marriage. About his desire to adopt the baby boy growing inside her.

He held out his hand. "Ready to get to the wedding? They said Daisy can come."

"What about Bessy and Jitterbug?"

"Funny you asked . . . because, last time I checked, they were actually standing near the fence, right behind that cross . . . almost like they knew about the ceremony and wanted to be a part of it."

She grinned and slipped her hand into his. "Sounds like them. I can't wait to see."

"Then let's go."

Teagan hadn't thought she would get a happy ending. But everything had fallen into place perfectly . . . and for that she was grateful.

~~~

If you enjoyed *Necessary Risk*, please consider leaving a review!

Keep reading for a preview of *Risky Ambition*.
~~~

USA TODAY BESTSELLING AUTHOR
CHRISTY BARRITT
Risky
AMBITION
VANISHING RANCH
VR
THE SERIES - BOOK THREE

RISKY AMBITION: CHAPTER ONE

Nate Casper, known as Ghost to his Navy friends, kept his aviator sunglasses over his eyes as he stood on the tarmac of the small, private air strip outside Los Angeles. His client should be here any time, and he was entirely more intrigued with his current flight assignment than he should be.

As a white SUV pulled through the gate, Wayne Stewart, his copilot, muttered, "Here goes nothing."

The vehicle came to a stop ten feet in front of them. A moment later, Chesney Blake stepped out wearing jeans, strappy heels, and a black, billowy blouse.

Ghost's breath caught at the sight of her.

The woman was undeniably beautiful with wavy dark hair that fell well below her shoulders, a Julia Roberts' smile, and expressive green eyes.

Everyone in the country—maybe even the world—thought so.

She was America's current movie star obsession.

And Ghost piloted her private flights.

Wayne leaned close while still maintaining a professional stance. "Remember to breathe."

Ghost offered a scoffing laugh. Was he *that* obvious?

"I don't know what you're talking about." Ghost raised his chin.

Any kind of relationship with Chesney was off-limits, both from a professional standpoint and a realistic one. Hollywood types seemed to be drawn to other Hollywood types—not to pilots.

Besides, his lifestyle and that of a movie star's?

They would never mesh.

Ghost's gaze remained on Chesney as she grabbed her suitcase from the back seat and began pulling it behind her as she walked toward the Cessna.

Today, there were no assistants with her. No manager or PR rep.

Only the person who'd driven her here.

Ghost squinted. Who *was* in the car with Chesney?

He waited.

As a pilot, his contract instructed him not to approach guests or get personal. But he hadn't always stuck by the rules.

This was his fifth flight with Chesney, and whenever Chesney had initiated a conversation—which she always did—he didn't back away.

His gaze traveled behind her as he tried to get a glimpse of the driver again.

He hoped she still wasn't hanging around with Damien Parrish.

Anger burned through Ghost's blood at the thought of the man.

Probably because Ghost had seen too many fights, too many bruises, too many tears.

Last time Ghost had flown with Chesney—probably nine months ago—he'd broken the rules.

He'd pulled her aside. Told her he could help. That she didn't have to live like this.

Chesney had simply listened, staring up at him with a broken look in her gaze. But there was no haughtiness. No condemnation toward him for not minding his own business.

Ghost had heard on the news several months ago that the two had broken up. He hoped the update was true.

As if in response to his thought, the driver's side door opened.

A man with slick blond hair, overblown biceps, and a permanent scowl stepped out into the mid-September day.

Damien.

Ghost's pulse pounded in his ears.

Had the two gotten back together?

Ghost felt his gaze darken.

The man had been Chesney's manager and then boyfriend. Damien liked to make headlines even more than Chesney—only the attention he got was because of his risky behavior. Partying. DUIs. Fights.

Ghost had no idea why Chesney could like someone

like Damien—unless she was the typical good girl who was drawn to bad boys.

Fighting a frown, Ghost plastered on a professional smile instead as the two approached the plane. This place was private, which was why most of their clients liked it—just the airstrip, some metal hangars, and a chain-link fence surrounding it all.

Now it was time to get down to business.

"Good afternoon, Ms. Blake and Mr. Parrish." Ghost shoved any personal thoughts aside as he started. "I know you've both flown with me before, but as a matter of procedure I'll go through the introductions. I'm your pilot, Nate Casper—but you can call me Ghost—and this is my copilot, Wayne Stewart. We're happy to have you flying with us. It looks like clear skies for travel today with a southwest wind at eight knots. It should be a smooth flight from LA to Miami. Do either of you have any questions before we take off?"

He glanced back and forth between Chesney and Damien.

Damien raised his head, dismissing Ghost with a flick of his gaze before slinging his leather bag over his shoulder. "No questions. We're wasting time here. Let's just go."

Another shot of irritation raced up Ghost's spine.

As Chesney stepped toward the plane, she leaned toward Ghost and whispered, "I'm so sorry he's acting like this."

Ghost wanted to tell her she had nothing to apologize for.

Instead, he offered a professional nod.

Before Chesney and Damien could climb the stairs to the Cessna, a car raced onto the runway. The dark sedan skidded to a stop about twenty feet away.

Ghost's muscles tensed as he watched, waiting to see who was inside and what they wanted.

The driver's side window rolled down probably two inches.

Then a dark, cylindrical object emerged from the slit.

His breath caught.

A gun.

"Get down!" Ghost dove for Chesney just as a barrage of bullets filled the air, littering everything within sight.

Still sheltering Chesney, Ghost reached for his phone and dialed 911.

They needed the police.

Now.

He quickly explained the situation to the operator before pocketing his phone and reaching for his gun. He almost always carried one with him. Just in case.

Ghost glanced back, desperate to see what the shooter's next move might be.

He didn't want to return fire, but he would if he had to.

His gaze stopped on Damien.

The man had ducked behind the airstairs.

Fear replaced his cool arrogance. But not necessarily surprise, Ghost realized.

This chaos was because of Damien, wasn't it?

More shots rang out.

Raising his own gun, Ghost fired a warning shot into the air.

The gunman retreated and raced away in his vehicle, his tires squealing.

Ghost tucked away his gun as his gaze shifted toward Wayne.

But he wasn't there.

Where had his friend gone?

Then he spotted his copilot lying on the asphalt . . . blood spreading across the shirt of his white uniform.

Ghost's lungs tightened.

His friend had been hit.

Horror washed through Chesney.

She hadn't been shot. But had anyone else?

They all could have died.

What was the pilot doing with a gun, anyway?

She didn't know, but she was thankful he'd had it and scared off the gunman.

Then she heard a guttural, "No!" come from Ghost.

He lifted himself off her and darted across the tarmac.

As he did, Chesney sat up, still feeling disoriented.

Then she saw the copilot.

On the ground.

Bloody.

The breath left her lungs.

She scrambled toward the two men, feeling a new urgency rush through her.

When she reached them, she saw that Wayne's face looked pale, almost lifeless. But raspy breaths continued to leave his lungs.

He was still alive, at least.

"He's losing a lot of blood." Ghost ripped off his jacket, balled it up, and placed it over Wayne's gunshot wound.

Chesney's heart continued to slam into her ribcage.

What had just happened was beginning to sink in.

Someone had shot at them.

Why?

Then the truth hit her.

Her gaze jerked toward Damien.

He still crouched behind the airstairs, phone to his ear.

Chesney would bet anything he *wasn't* calling the police.

No, whatever he was doing, it was in an effort to look out for his own interests.

Like he always did.

Chesney turned her attention back to Ghost, desperate to help. "What can I do?"

"Hold this." He nodded toward his jacket. "Put as much pressure on the wound as you can. We've got to stop Wayne from losing any more blood."

Ghost wanted *her* to stop his copilot's bleeding?

Apprehension fluttered through her. "I . . . I don't know if I can."

Ghost's gaze locked with hers. "You can do it, Chesney. I know you can."

Chesney shoved aside her self-doubt. As Ghost directed, she placed her hands over Wayne's wound and pressed down as hard as she could.

Ghost stood, his muscles rigid as if ready to spring into action.

"What's wrong?" More panic raced through her, and she glanced around. "Is the guy coming back?"

"I don't see his vehicle. I have to make sure the ambulance can find us. I hear the sirens in the distance. But our GPS coordinates online are wrong."

Now that he mentioned it, Chesney heard the wailing sirens too. The sound was getting closer.

Thank God.

Ghost stepped toward the gate, then seemed to hesitate as he looked back at her. It was almost as if he feared she was still in danger.

"I'm okay." Chesney pressed the jacket over Wayne's chest. "Just go. Make sure help gets here in time."

With a nod, he turned and jogged toward the gate.

Mere seconds after Ghost left, Damien appeared beside her. His gaze skittered around them, and sweat lined his upper lip. "We need to get out of here."

"What do you mean get out of here?" Outrage shot through Chesney as the implications of what he said fell on her. "We can't just let this man bleed to death."

"I'm telling you—we need to leave." Damien

nodded toward her SUV, his words coming out fast—almost breathless. "Now."

"I can't leave. This man's life depends on me." Her gaze narrowed as she studied her former boyfriend. "Who was that guy, Damien?"

"It doesn't matter." He glanced around again, his motions frantic. "As long as he doesn't come back. But he might. Or someone else might come. I don't know. No one was supposed to know I was here."

Chesney pictured Ghost rushing toward the gate to flag down the ambulance.

What if that guy *did* come back? Ghost would be a target if that was the case.

Her gaze met Damien's. "If you think this guy or his friends might return, you need to warn Ghost before someone else is hurt."

"There's no time for that. I need to get you out of here. Now. Your safety is my first concern."

Chesney wanted to snort at his sad attempt of chivalry. Clearly, that wasn't true. More times than she could count, Damien had been the reason her safety was on the line.

Another gurgling sound left Wayne, and she remembered his condition, feeling foolish to be arguing right now while this man's life was at risk.

"I'm not leaving." She shook her head. "I've got to help this man."

Damien's gaze darkened as he fisted and unfisted his hands.

For a moment—and just a moment—she wondered if he'd grab her and force her to leave with him.

She braced herself for an argument or fight.

Finally, Damien reached into his pocket and pulled out her car keys. "Fine. Have it your way. But I'm out of here. I'd watch your back if I were you."

Chesney's mouth dropped open as she watched Damien jog toward her SUV. He climbed inside and squealed away—leaving Chesney, Wayne, and Ghost stranded.

Damien was the one that the gunman was after, wasn't he?

So why did Chesney need to watch her back also?

As Wayne let out another raspy gasp, Chesney's thoughts turned back to the situation.

She had to do everything within her power to make sure this man didn't die because of Damien's poor decisions.

Read More Here!

ALSO BY CHRISTY BARRITT:

FOG LAKE SUSPENSE

Edge of Peril

When evil descends like fog on a mountain community, no one feels safe. After hearing about a string of murders in a Smoky Mountain town, journalist Harper Jennings realizes a startling truth. She knows who may be responsible—the same person who tried to kill her three years ago. Now Harper must convince the cops to believe her before the killer strikes again. Sheriff Luke Wilder returned to his hometown, determined to keep the promise he made to his dying father. The sleepy tourist area with a tragic past hadn't seen a murder in decades—until now. Keeping the community safe seems impossible as darkness edges closer, threatening to consume everything in its path. As The Watcher grows desperate, Harper and Luke must work together in order to defeat him. But the peril around them escalates, making it clear the killer will stop at nothing to get what he wants.

Margin of Error

Some secrets have deadly consequences. Brynlee Parker thought her biggest challenge would be hiking to Dead Man's Bluff and fulfilling her dad's last wishes. She never thought she'd witness two men being viciously murdered while on a mountainous trail. Even worse, the deadly predator is now hunting her. Boone Wilder wants nothing to do with Dead Man's Bluff, not after his wife died there. But he can't seem to mind his own business when a mysterious out-of-towner burst into his camp store in a frenzied panic. Something—or someone—deadly is out there. The killer's hunger for blood seems to be growing at a brutal pace. Can Brynlee and Boone figure out who's behind these murders? Or will the hurts and secrets from their past not allow for even a margin of error?

Brink of Danger

Ansley Wilder has always lived life on the wild side, using thrills to numb the pain from her past and escape her mistakes. But a near-death experience two years ago changed everything. When another incident nearly claims her life, she turns her thrill-seeking ways into a fight for survival. Ryan Philips left Fog Lake to chase adventure far from home. Now he's returned as the new fire chief in town, but the slower paced life he seeks is nowhere to be found. Not only is a wildfire blazing out of control, but a malicious killer known as "The Woodsman" is enacting crimes that appear accidental. Plus, there seems to be a strange connection with these incidents and his best friend's little sister, Ansley Wilder. As a killer watches their every move and the forest fire threatens to destroy their scenic town, both Ryan and Ansley hover on the brink of danger. One wrong move could send them tumbling over the edge . . . permanently.

Line of Duty

Jaxon Wilder didn't plan on returning home to Fog Lake, Tennessee, following his tour of duty in Iraq. But after a gut-wrenching failure during his stint in the Army, he now faces a new challenge: his family. Abby Brennan always did her best to be the good girl and to live by the rules. When a wrong decision changes her entire life, she tries to hide from the world. However, a madman known as the Executioner is determined to find her and enact his own brand of justice. When Jaxon and Abby are thrown together in the killer's crosshairs, they're forced to depend on one another to survive. Will Jaxon's sense of duty be enough to help keep Abby safe? Or will deadly secrets lead to the penalty of death?

Legacy of Lies

The justice system failed her family—and so did her hometown. Madison Colson knows deep down that her father—a convicted serial killer—is innocent. But believing it and proving it are two entirely different things. Unable to help her father, Madison has spent most of her adult life overcompensating by helping others. When her aunt dies unexpectantly, duty calls her back to Fog Lake, Tennessee, a beautiful but painful place she'd rather forget. Terrifying events begin to unfold once she arrives, unleashing her worst night-mares. The Good Samaritan Killer—or a copycat—is back, and now Madison Colson is his target. FBI Special Agent Shane Townsend is determined to stop the deadly rampage that has sent the tightknit community into a frenzy. But he needs to earn Madison's trust first. The task feels impossible, especially considering his father is the one who put her dad in prison. With the whole town on edge and pointing fingers, tension esca-lates out of control. Madison and Shane must sort the facts from the lies—and fight for a legacy of truth—before The Good Samaritan Killer has the final say.

Secrets of Shame

A killer has a promise to keep . . . Attorney Isaac Colson only wants to put his tumultuous past in Fog Lake behind him and return to his life in Memphis. But when an ominous text threatens that he must come back or there will be deadly consequences, he knows he can't take any chances. Rebecca Moreno has only ever loved one man—her high school sweetheart, Isaac Colson. But when his dad went to prison for murder, Rebecca's father forbade them from seeing each other again. Years later, Isaac is back in town and old feelings are stirring. But Rebecca is harboring a secret that could change everything. When The Good Samaritan Killer strikes again, guilt pummels her. She has to tell Isaac the truth.

But as events unfold, she has more to lose than ever. Isaac and Rebecca must find answers—their lives depend on it. But everyone seems to have secrets, each that forms an obstacle to finding the truth . . . and to staying alive.

Refuge of Redemption

Home is a place of refuge—unless it's a killer's playground. For years, Bear Colson has been known as the serial killer's son. But now, someone else is behind bars for the crimes his father was accused of committing. Bear wants to believe hope for a brighter future is in sight, but he has reason to suspect more than one killer was involved. Forensic photographer Piper Stephens' career crashed and burned when she trusted the wrong man. Now, after discovering an alarming secret about the infamous Good Samaritan Killer, she sets out to find both answers and redemption. But things go awry when her assistant becomes the next victim. As fear batters Fog Lake residents once again, Bear and Piper join forces to track down the truth. But the killer is determined to remain in the shadows—and he'll destroy anyone who stands in his way.

ABOUT THE AUTHOR

USA Today has called Christy Barritt's books "scary, funny, passionate, and quirky."

Christy writes both mystery and romantic suspense novels that are clean with underlying messages of faith. Her books have won the Daphne du Maurier Award for Excellence in Suspense and Mystery, have been twice nominated for the Romantic Times Reviewers' Choice Award, and have finaled for both a Carol Award and Foreword Magazine's Book of the Year.

She is married to her Prince Charming, a man who thinks she's hilarious—but only when she's not trying to be. Christy is a self-proclaimed klutz, an avid music lover who's known for spontaneously bursting into song, and a road trip aficionado.

When she's not working or spending time with her family, she enjoys singing, playing the guitar, and exploring small, unsuspecting towns where people have no idea how accident-prone she is.

Find Christy online at:

www.christybarritt.com
www.facebook.com/christybarritt
www.twitter.com/cbarritt

Sign up for Christy's newsletter to get information on all of her latest releases here: **www.christybarritt.com/ newsletter-sign-up/**